Born in Denver on April 8, 1909, John Fante migrated to Los Angeles in his early twenties. Classically out of place in a town built on celluloid dreams, Fante's literary fiction was full of torn grace and redemptive vengeance. His first novel, *Wait Until Spring, Bandini* was published in 1938, and it was in the following year that *Ask the Dust* appeared (both novels are also published by Canongate, as well as *The Road to Los Angeles*).

Fante was stricken with diabetes in 1955 and its complications brought about blindness in 1978, but he continued to write by dictation to his wife, Joyce. He died at the age of 74 on May 8, 1983.

1933 Was A Bad Year

John Fante

CANONGATE

First published in the UK in 2001 by Canongate Books,
14 High Street, Edinburgh EH1 1TE

10 9 8 7 6 5 4 3 2 1

British Library Cataloguing-in-Publication Data
A catalogue record for this book is available upon request
from the British Library.

ISBN 1 84195 192 7

Typeset by Palimpsest Book Production Limited,
Polmont, Stirlingshire

Printed and bound by Omnia Books Ltd, Glasgow.

1933 WAS A BAD YEAR

Chapter One

It was a bad one, the winter of 1933. Wading home that night through flames of snow, my toes burning, my ears on fire, the snow swirling around me like a flock of angry nuns, I stopped dead in my tracks. The time had come to take stock. Fair weather or foul, certain forces in the world were at work trying to destroy me.

Dominic Molise, I said, hold it. Is everything going according to plan? Examine your condition with care, take an impartial survey of your situation. What goes on here, Dom?

There I was in Roper, Colorado, growing older by the minute. In six months I would be eighteen and graduated from high school. I was sixty-four inches tall and had not grown one centimeter in three years. I was bowlegged and pigeon-toed and my ears protruded like Pinocchio's. My teeth were crooked, and my face was as freckled as a bird's egg.

I was the son of a bricklayer who had not worked in five months. I didn't own an overcoat, I wore three sweaters, and my mother had already begun a series of novenas for the new suit I needed to graduate in June.

Lord, I said, for in those days I was a believer who spoke frankly to his God: Lord, what gives? Is this what you want? Is this why you put me on the earth? I didn't *ask* to be born.

I had absolutely nothing to do with it, except that I'm here, asking fair questions, the reasons why, so tell me, give me a sign: is this my reward for trying to be a good Christian, for twelve years of Catholic doctrine and four years of Latin? Have I ever doubted the Transubstantiation, or the Holy Trinity, or the Resurrection? How many Masses have I missed on Sundays and holy days of obligation? Lord, you can count them on your fingers.

Are you playing a game with me? Have things gotten out of hand? Have you lost control? Is Lucifer back in power? Be honest with me, for I'm troubled all the time. Give me a clue. Is life worth while? Will everything turn out right?

We lived on Arapahoe Street, at the foot of the first hills that rose to become the eastern slope of the Rocky Mountains. They shot up like jagged skyscrapers, staring down at our town, a haze of blue and green in summer, sugar-white in winter, with peaked turrets shrouded in the clouds. Every winter someone was lost up there, trapped in a canyon or buried in a snowslide. In spring the melting snows turned Roper Creek into a wild river that swept away fences and bridges and flooded the streets, piling mud along Pearl Street and inundating the courthouse basement. Cold country, bad-tempered country, the earth's crust a sheet of ice through April, snow on Easter Sunday, sometimes a sudden snowstorm in May: bad country for a ballplayer, specially for a pitcher who hadn't thrown a ball since October.

But The Arm kept me going, that sweet left arm, the one nearest my heart. The snow couldn't hurt it and the wind couldn't pierce it because I kept it soaked with Sloan's Liniment, a little bottle of it in my pocket at all times, I reeked with it, sometimes sent out of class to wash the pine tartness away, but I walked out proudly without shame, conscious of my destiny, steeled against the sneers of the boys and the tilted nostrils of the girls.

I had a great stride in those days, the gait of a gunslinger, the looseness of the classic lefthander, the left shoulder drooping a little, The Arm dangling limp as a serpent — my arm, my blessed, holy arm that came from God, and if The Lord created me out of a poor bricklayer he hung me with jewels when he hinged that whizzer to my collarbone.

Let it snow then! And let the winters be long and cold with spring a time to dream about, for this was not the end of Dominic Molise after all, only his beginning, and the warm summer sun would find him doing the work of God with his cunning left arm. This snow-swept Arapahoe Street was a place of distinction, a landmark where once he walked on despairing nights, his birthplace, to be so inscribed in the Hall of Fame. A plaque, if you please, a bronze plaque set in concrete on a monument at the corner of Ninth and Arapahoe Streets: Boyhood Neighborhood of Dominic Molise, World's Greatest Southpaw.

God had answered my questions, cleared my doubts, restored my faith, and the world was right again. The wind vanished and the snow drifted down like hushed confetti. Grandma Bettina used to say that snowflakes were the souls in heaven returning to Earth for brief visits. I knew this was not true but it was possible, and I believed it sometimes when the whim amused me.

I held out my hand and many flakes fell upon it, alive and star-shaped for a few seconds, and who could say? Perhaps the soul of Grandpa Giovanni, dead seven years now, and Joe Hardt, our third baseman, killed last summer on his motorcycle, and all of my father's people in the faraway mountains of Abruzzi, great-aunts and uncles I had never known, all vanished from the earth. And the others, the billions who lived a while and went away, the poor soldiers killed in battle, the sailors lost at sea, the victims of plague and earthquake, the rich and the poor, the dead from the beginning of time, none escaping except Jesus Christ, the only one in all the history of man who ever came back, but no one else, and did I believe that?

I had to believe it. Where did my slider come from, and my knuckle-ball, and where did I get all that control? If I stopped believing I might come apart, lose my rhythm, start walking batters. Hell yes, there were doubts, but I pushed them back. The life of a pitcher was tough enough without losing faith in his God. One flash of doubt might bring a crimp in The Arm, so why muddy the water? Leave things alone. The Arm came from heaven. Believe that. Never mind predestination, and if God is all good how come so much evil, and if he knows everything how come he created people and sent them to hell? Plenty of time for that. Get into the minors, move up to the big time, pitch in the World Series, make the Hall of Fame. *Then* sit back and ask questions, ask what does God look like, and why are babies born crippled, and who made hunger and death.

Through the whispering snow I saw dimly the small houses along Arapahoe. I knew everyone in every house, every cat and dog in the neighborhood. In truth I knew almost everyone of Roper's ten thousand people, and some day they would all be dead. That too was the fate of everyone in the house at the end of the street, the frame house with the sagging front porch, paint-blistered, with the slanting peaked roof, home of bricklayer Peter Molise, where the only bricks were in the chimney, and even that was crumbling.

But when it was time to die the condition of your house didn't matter, and all of us would have to go — Grandma Bettina next, then Papa, then Mama, then myself since I was the oldest, then my brother August, two years younger, then my sister Clara, and finally my little brother Frederick. Somewhere along the way our dog Rex would crawl off and die too.

Why was I thinking these things and making a graveyard of the world? Was I losing my faith after all? Could it be because I was poor? Impossible. All great ballplayers came from poor folks. Who ever heard of a rich rookie becoming a Ty Cobb or a Babe Ruth! Was it a girl? There were no girls in my life, except Dorothy Parrish, who hardly knew I existed, a mere gnat in her life.

Oh, God, help me! And I walked faster, my thoughts pursuing me, and I began to run, my frozen shoes squealing like mice, but running didn't help, the thoughts to the left and right and behind me. But as I ran, The Arm, that good left arm, took hold of the situation and spoke soothingly: ease up, Kid, it's loneliness, you're all alone in the world; your father, your mother, your faith, they can't help you, nobody helps anybody, you only help yourself, and that's why I'm here, because we are inseparable, and we'll take care of everything.

Oh, Arm! Strong and faithful arm, talk sweetly to me now. Tell me of my future, the crowds cheering, the pitch sliding across at the knees, the batters coming up and going down, fame and fortune and victory, we shall have it all. And one day we shall die and lie side by side in a grave, Dom

Molise and his beautiful arm, the sports world shocked, in mourning, the telegram to my family from the President of the United States, the flags at half-mast at every ball park in the nation, fans weeping unashamed, Damon Runyon's four-part biography in the *Saturday Evening Post*: Triumph over Adversity, the Life of Dominic Molise.

Under an elm tree I stopped to cry, the bitterness of my approaching death too much to bear; one so young, so talented, cut down in the prime of his life. Oh God, be merciful: don't take me too fast! Spare me a few years, look kindly upon my youth. By nineteen I shall be ready for the big time. Give me those years and ten more, a total of twelve, no more and no less, I don't care if it's with the Phillies or the Cubs, only give me those years and you can strike me down at twenty-nine, which is plenty of time, my sweet Lord, figuring thirty games a year, that's three hundred and sixty games, a lot of baseball, a lot of pitches to emblazon the name of Dom Molise among the immortals.

The house was in darkness, the front windows staring blind-eyed. The clean untrod snow upon the path meant Papa was still down at the Onyx, shooting pool.

I kicked the snow from my shoes and stepped into the front room where Clara slept on the sofa and Frederick on an army cot. It was a crowded house. The only one with a private bedroom was Grandma Bettina, and hers was hardly a bedroom, a tiny place with a slanting roof off the kitchen, where the bed took up all the space and left no room for even a chair.

I turned on the kitchen light, put a match to the oven in the gas stove, and got out my homework – history, a paragraph of Virgil to translate, and the writing of a short essay on the mystical body of Christ. It was one of those easier nights when Sister Mary Delphine, wearying of pouring it on, gave us a breather.

Even so, it took an hour to translate six lines of Latin, and at midnight I started the essay on the mystical body of Christ.

'What is the mystical body of Christ?' I began. 'A good question, an important question, so important that, if we know nothing else, it is sufficient to sustain us to the very gates of Heaven. And since it is so important, then we must put our full attention to it. All important dogma deserves our deepest reflection. Too often we forget this, and many a sinner in his final hours before the last judgement stands regretful before God Almighty, trembling in fear and regret for having neglected the truths of his faith. If we would but study the dogma of our blessed church as much as we waste time reading trashy books and seeing obscene motion pictures in order to consider the mystical body of Christ, then our salvation would be assured. Time is short and the hour cometh. Our Lord asks very little of his creatures. He has provided us with unselfish teachers, the blessed nuns of the Order of St Catherine, and too often we fail to realize what a golden opportunity is given us to take advantage of their wisdom and advice. So let us heed the sacred counsel of our beloved sisters and think carefully of the meaning of the mystical body of Christ. The sins of the world are many, alas, but no sinner is greater than he who neglects the study of our holy faith, and when we are called to account some day for the offenses in this life, let us hope that we will not be charged with turning our eyes from the sacred truths of God's holy church.'

Bull's eye.

The essay would bring an A plus. No matter if it didn't explain the mystical body of Christ, no matter if it was laced with nonsense, all the beguiling phrases were there, irresistible to Sister Mary Delphine: 'regretful before Almighty God – trembling in fear – trashy books – obscene motion pictures – the blessed nuns of the Order of St Catherine – the sacred truths of God's holy church.' Delphine would cream in her pants.

I was studying history when the squeal of bedsprings seeped from Bettina's room. Grandma Bettina, deadly enemy of the light company, came to the kitchen door in her flannel nightgown. She was a small fierce old lady with hands so fleshless they seemed like claws clasped upon the small mound of her tummy. Her hair was white as linen, the skin at her temples so pale and transparent you could almost see inside her head. She spoke only Italian and pretended not to understand English whenever the subject matter displeased her.

For ten seconds she just stood there, nodding at me with a despondent smile.

'There he sits,' she kept nodding. 'The brilliant young American, the product of an American womb, the pride of his dim-witted mother, the hope of the coming generation, there he sits, burning electricity.'

'Grandma, I'm trying to study.'

'And what are you studying, O wise and clever grandson? Is it a book about hunger and men walking the streets seeking work? Is it a book telling of your father without a job for seven months, or is it the rich promise of golden America, land of equality and brotherhood, beautiful America, stinking like a plague?'

'We're having a depression,' I told her. 'Besides, it's winter. Papa can't lay brick in this weather.'

She clasped her hands in front of her.

'How clever are the young Americans!' she breathed, rocking her hands. 'The generation with all the answers!'

I groaned.

She sniffed the air, the Sloan's Liniment.

'As always, you smell like a pestilence.'

'It's a clean smell.'

'The smell of a sick country. Hear my words: one day this stench will cover all the land.'

She was launched.

'Who do you deceive with those foolish books?' she wanted to know, a lawyer showing off in court. 'Better that you should fall on your knees and pray for mercy!' Her mouth was at my ear, her nose in my hair as she whispered a leering question: 'Have you been to confession lately? Any boy of seventeen should go at least twice a day.'

That did it.

'Old woman, drop dead!'

'Ha!' she barked. 'Young America speaks, showing its respect for the aged! At last I come to my reward for bringing your father into the world! For this I traveled five thousand miles in steerage to a barbarian land!' The insults came like buckshot: I was a jackal, a rat, a snake, a monster out of the belly of my mother. I was deformed, an elbow grew out of the back of my head, my nose was at my navel, my eyes were in my ass. My mother was a donkey, a cow, a pig, a chicken, a she-goat. Her people were cowards, thieves, whores, lunatics who would finish their days in an insane asylum. As for me, I would end up with a rope around my neck at a public hanging, alongside my two brothers. America would go down in flames, set afire by exploding light companies.

Swift as an old cat she crossed to the naked light bulb over the table and snapped it off, then swished away to her room and slammed the door. I turned on the light and heard her in there, crying out to God.

'Release me from this bondage. Put me in a box and send me back to Torricella Peligna!'

I knew her troubled soul, and I pitied her. She was lonely, her roots dangling in an alien land. She had not wanted to come to America, but my grandfather had given her no other choice. There had been poverty in Abruzzi too, but it was a sweeter poverty that everyone shared like bread passed around. Death was shared too, and grief, and good times, and the village of Torricella Peligna was like a single human being. My grandmother was a finger torn from the rest of the body and nothing in the new life could assuage her desolation. She was like all those others who had come from her part of Italy. Some were better off, and some were wealthy, but the joy was gone from their lives, and the new country was a lonely place where 'O Sole Mio' and 'Come Back to Sorrento' were heartbreak songs.

Bettina's cries now brought my mother from her bedroom, her thick brown hair hanging to her waist, her hands clutching her nightgown. Her eyes were enormous and green and always astonished. She was born in Chicago, but she was of Italian stock and really a peasant like Grandma, the mark of loneliness upon her too, inexpressibly alien, not Italian and far less American, a fragile misfit. Her people were from Potenza, a town above Naples, a place reputed to be full of redheads.

In Grandma Bettina's opinion, the Potenzese, next to Americans, were the most ridiculous people in the world. Not that Grandma had ever been to Potenza and seen it with her own eyes, but all her life she had heard wild stories about the Potenzese.

Since the Abruzzese had need of a place they considered beneath their own, they settled on Potenza in the manner that the Calabrese despised the Sicilians, and the Neapolitans scorned everything south of Naples, and the Romans tilted their noses at the Neapolitans, and the Florentines shrugged off the Romans. To the Abruzzese, the people of Potenza were some kind of a national joke, as if they lived in tilted houses and were all dwarfs. Just mentioning Potenza always brought a condescending smirk from my father. He had married the daughter of the Potenzese, God help him, but he was always ready to smile patiently at this ironic turn of events, and only too glad to forgive his wife for her parents.

Listening at Bettina's door to the last of the old woman's laments, Mama clicked her tongue patiently, for the Potenzese looked down on the Abruzzese too.

'She means well, the poor old thing. She's had such a hard life . . . all those people.'

'What people?'

'From Abruzzi. No wonder they're rough and badtempered. It's nothing but rocks and a few goats and no electric lights. Like Calabria and Sicily and all those poor places.'

She had never been there, had never been anywhere except a Chicago tenement.

'How do you know?'

'Everybody knows. You can tell by the way they act,

yelling, swearing, fighting. It's in their blood. Look at your father.'

She moved closer, smelling of sleep, a fragrant mustiness, talcum powder and soap and the top drawer of her dresser with the sachet bags. Sometimes when I could not sleep I went into her bedroom and exchanged pillows with her and the fragrance worked like a drug. She was so much older than her forty years. It was hard to think that she had ever been young. There was a photograph of her at ten, sitting in a swing at a Chicago playground, and she looked forty there too, a little girl of forty with pig-tails and white shoes.

She crossed to the sink and poured a cup of water, drinking it slowly because it was so cold, and I could hear it tumbling into her.

'Were you downtown tonight?' she asked.

'I went to the show. I didn't see him.'

'Who?' she asked, innocently.

'Papa.'

'He lost ten dollars last night.'

If my father admitted losing ten it must have been more like fifty. It was his pool-playing that kept us going during the winter. He was far and away the best billiard player in Roper, but his skill went against him because it was hard to lure competitors, and he had to give away too many points. Sharp as he was in calculating the talents of a stranger, he sometimes ran into a hustler from Denver or Cheyenne who would wipe him out. Then he would start over again, playing for quarters and half dollars, sometimes borrowing to get off the ground and build another stake.

'Do women go there?' Mama asked.

She constantly asked it, and I always said no, but she knew

otherwise. The Onyx was a wide open saloon with a bar in front and the pool and poker tables behind the partition to the rear. Women were barred from the back room, but at the bar they were as numerous as the men.

'It's a bad part of town,' she said. 'I'd be afraid to go in there.'

'What's bad about it? The police station is right across the street.'

'That's true,' she said, staring, something else disturbing her.

I knew. She could not bring herself to express it: that she suspected my father of playing around. It seemed such a corny notion – old Papa, the father of four children, a bricklayer out of work and trying to hustle a buck with a cue stick, taking on the added trouble of another woman. The plain truth was, my father didn't like women very much. Not even his own mother, and certainly not his wife.

'What's wrong with him?' she went on. 'I'll never under-stand it. A nice home, four wonderful children, spaghetti on the table, wine in the cellar, and he's out every night. Even if he doesn't care for me, you'd think he'd have some consideration for his children. Why does a man do that?'

'It's very simple. He hates women and children. Besides, where would we be if he didn't scratch out a few dollars shooting pool?'

'All the time? Day and night, Sundays too? Not even to Mass once in a while? Nobody shoots pool that much.'

'It's the way he is, and you can't change it.'

'He'll change. God'll step in one of these days. You'll see.'

She meant her prayers, the peeling of thousands of rosary

beads through thousands of days on her knees in the locked bedroom. There were lumps on her kneecaps telling of it.

She eased quietly behind me and I felt her cold fingers through my hair, and then her hands palming my mushroom ears.

'Don't,' I said, squirming away.

'Wear the stocking. And keep praying.'

The remedy for protruding ears, as suggested by the Potenzese, was the wearing of a woman's stocking over your head at night. It worked fine until you removed the stocking. Then the ears sprang out again.

'I've learned to live with my ears, Mama. Will you please try to do the same?'

'But have you *tried* the Blessed Mother? Try her for a month. If she can make cripples walk, look how easy for her to ...'

'Shut up!' I screamed. 'Leave me alone, leave my ears alone!'

She stared, wounded, large-eyed, and without a word she turned and walked quietly back to the bedroom, her troubled spirit dragging after her like a tattered wedding veil.

I was sorry I had screamed at her, I hated myself, but the idea of praying to the mother of God to flatten my ears, since her son had made them stick out in the first place, seemed like plain madness. Prayer! What good was it? What had it done for her? My father beside her in bed every night, listening to the click of her rosary, finding her on her knees, shivering in the cold, what the hell are you doing down there, come to bed for Christ's sake before you freeze to death, her prayers a snapping whip at his ass, reminding him of his worthlessness, his wife like a child writing letters to Santa Claus, collapsing from life into the arms of God, of St Teresa, of the Virgin Mary. Oh, my mother was a good woman, a noble woman, she never cheated or lied or deceived *or* ever spoke an unkind word. She scrubbed floors and hung out huge bundles of laundry and ironed by the hour, she cooked and sewed and swept and smiled bravely at hard times, God's victim, my father's victim, her children's victim, she walked about with the wounds of Christ in her hands and feet, a crown of thorns about her head. Her suffering was too unbearable to watch, so that I wished she'd say oh shit, or fuck it Jasper, or piss on you Joe. I longed for the day of revolt when she would break a wine jug over my father's head, smack Bettina in the mouth and beat us children with a stick. But she punished us instead with Our Fathers and Hail Marys, she strangled us with a string of rosary beads.

Prayer. Oh, prayers! Oh, the reaching out into nothingness for small favors like a pair of shoes, or miracles like adding another six inches to my height so that I could develop a really fast ball. Years of prayers – and what was the result? I had even stopped measuring myself against the bedroom wall. The futility of it! If St Francis of Assisi, one of the princes of the Church, was only five feet tall, then what chance had I of reaching six feet? Hell, it was a total waste of time, a gnashing of teeth in the wilderness.

The old clock on the stove clucked away and it was after one when I finished studying. The house was cold now, an icy cold that crept into the kitchen from under the floors. I heard something, a step or a sigh, and looked out into the backyard. The world was as white and silent as the moon. Snow mounds outlined rows of cabbages buried in straw in the garden. Slowly I felt a presence, something out there and all around the house, an energy alive and unseen, ominous as a burglar, trying to break in, peering through every window, pushing against doors and walls. I knew what it was, and I was afraid to think of it.

I turned from the window and got the big bottle of Sloan's from the dish cabinet. I poured a generous handful and massaged the piney tartness into The Arm, rubbing and pressing and kneading it into the flesh. I smeared it on my chest and neck and dabbed my nostrils until I felt calm again and the pain had burned me fearless.

What a problem! Was this the way it was going to be? Other people had thoughts of death, and each put them down in his own way. I couldn't rely on The Arm forever, dousing it with liniment. It made for a very dubious future. What would happen if I got lost in the mountains for a week, alone and without Sloan's? I saw myself screaming, running mad through the forest.

Far down the street, the sound carrying boldly in the frozen stillness, came footsteps quick and crunching the snow. It had to be my father. He always walked with determination and purpose, going nowhere. The front porch shook as he stomped the snow from his shoes.

'That damn stuff,' I heard him grumble as he stepped into the front room and sniffed. He stomped through the house, his way of informing everyone that he had arrived, and found me at the kitchen sink, the bottle of liniment in my hand.

'When you gonna grow up?' he said, his nostrils quivering.

His cheeks shone like apples. He hung his hat and overcoat on a hook behind the door. He was forty-five, with massive hands and short thick fingers. He was a neat man, careful of his dress, and even in work clothes he looked spruced up because of the white neckties he liked to wear, and the small mustache he kept meticulously trimmed. He wore a thick silver ring on the index finger of his left hand which he claimed was the secret to his skill with a pool cue. Though he was seldom at home, except for eating and sleeping, the house had an unmistakable way of jolting to attention, like an engine starting up, the moment he came through the door.

I watched him dig the stub of a cigar from his shirt pocket and sink his teeth into it as he poured wine from a jug into a saucepan. He not only smoked cigars, he ate them up, bit by bit. He put a match to the gas burner and placed the pan over the blue flame. Then he dropped a couple of bay leaves into the wine. He stared at it in silence, waiting for it to heat up.

'Papa,' I said. 'Do you ever think about dying?'

He looked at me in surprise.

'What kind of a question is that?'

'Well, *do* you?'

'What for?'

'No reason. But doesn't it pop into your head once in a while?'

'Never.'

'Never?'

'Never. Don't think about it. Think about living. Think about school. How you doin' in school?'

'I'm passing. I'll graduate.'

'Then what?'

'I don't know. I'm considering it.'

'What?'

'My career.'

'What career?'

'My future.'

'What future?'

'Numerous possibilities.'

'Baseball,' he said. 'Phooey.'

'Did I make a reference to baseball?'

'You know Johnny Di Massio?'

I knew him, a bricklayer compatriot of my father's, also a pool shark.

'Fastest, cleanest bricklayer in the state. Left-handed too, like you.'

'The similarity does not overwhelm me,' I said, putting him down, since he spoke cautious and uncertain English.

'Some day you're gonna be faster than Johnny.'

It was a shock. I lifted my left hand to the light. 'You're asking me to use *this* for laying brick? Surely you can't be serious, sir.'

'Sure I'm serious. I'll learn you the trade. Three, four years mixing mortar and carrying the hod, and you'll be up on the scaffold with me. We'll be partners – father and son, contractors, figuring jobs together. Make money.'

For years he had tried to interest me in bricklaying. His father and grandfathers for generations had been bricklayers and masons, and he believed the trade was planted in the blood line, blossoming with every new generation. When I was only seven he took me to the job for the first time and I got a nickel a day carrying drinking water to the bricklayers. The past two summers I had worked for him as a helper, operating a concrete mixer and packing a hod. It had been donkey work, and The Arm resented it and was sore all the time.

He himself was a very good bricklayer, laying them as expertly as he shot pool, fast and neat and with a rhythm, but he stayed poor just the same, no matter how hard he worked, until it was plain that being poor was not his fault but the fault of his trade.

I tried to speak calmly, reasonably, respectful of his temper, which could explode like a bullet.

'Papa,' I said. 'I regret to say this, but I don't think I have the right temperament for bricklaying.'

'Temperament – what's temperament got to do with it? Just put one brick on top of another and keep your wall plumb. Any jackass can do it.'

'My talent lies in other areas.'

'What talent?'

'A special talent. You might say I was born with it.'

He gave me a look of disgust, grabbed a glass tumbler from the cupboard and slammed it on the table. Then he poured the mulled wine into it, blowing on the wine to cool it, glaring at me.

'What talent?' he repeated.

I wanted to speak the truth but it wasn't in me to say baseball. He still swung at me now and then, missing on purpose, but you could never be sure.

'Medicine,' I said. 'Helping sick people get well, crippled little children, people with heart trouble and dropsy.'

The anger left his face and he was thoughtful as he sipped the steaming wine. 'That takes money,' he said.

'And time.'

'How long?'

'Eight years of college.'

'You better think of something else. I can't afford it. My

God, Kid, you're almost eighteen years old! When I was your age I was cutting stone.'

'I won't lay brick.'

He sighed and sat down.

'Look, Kid,' he said, running his fingers through his hair. 'I know what's eating you, but you don't have to quit baseball. You can play with the Plasterers' Union. They got a good team. Sunday ball is plenty.'

'Oh, great. Lay brick all week long, bust my fingers, and pitch on Sundays. It's the best offer I've had in years.'

He shook his head patiently, cupping the wine tumbler in both hands and breathing on it, keeping his eyes averted.

'We're in trouble,' he said quietly. 'We owe everybody — the rent, the lights, the gas, the butcher, the doctor, the bank, the lumber yard.' His brown eyes came up as if from a deep pool and implored me to understand.

It was not an easy admission of crisis. He was a proud man with faith in himself and in good times and he kept his problems hidden as well as possible for a poor man. He had never asked for help before. I looked at him and saw a lonely man with a houseful of kids and no way out. He would never own more than the clothes on his back, his sack of mason's tools, his concrete-mixer, and his favorite pool cue. He would go on working year after year until his strength gave out, until he could stoop no more over a wall, and the trowel fell from his hand. Why had he come so far, all the way from Abruzzi, for this? Grandma Bettina was right. He should have stayed in the old country. Had he done so, it would have changed my life too. What did they play in Torricella Peligna — soccer, bocci?

'I'll help, Papa.'

'Good boy,' taking a big gulp of the mulled wine. 'This June you graduate. Then we'll go to work. We'll show them! Show the whole world. Father and son. We'll pay our debts, save our money, and some day we'll go in the lumber business.'

'Lumber business?' I stared.

'That's where the money is.'

'Pass, Papa. I'll learn to lay brick, but I want no part of the lumber business.'

'Not right now. In the future. Four, five years of laying brick, then the lumber business.'

'But why the lumber business? Isn't laying brick bad enough?'

'That's what I mean. A man should work hard to get out of it. But it's a trade, a start.'

So there it was. The whole book. The Tragic Life of Dominic Molise, written by his father. Part One: The Thrills of Bricklaying. Part Two: Fun in a Lumber Yard. Part Three: How To Let Your Father Ruin Your Life. Part Four: Here Lies Dominic Molise, Obedient Son.

I mulled it over and decided not to argue, not at that hour. I just sat there soothing my arm, stroking it, calming it down as it whimpered like a child.

Papa drained the tumbler and daubed his mustache with a knuckle, his face to the light for the first time. It was then that I noticed it, a scarlet smear on his upper lip below the mustache. I couldn't help staring, and he sensed my surprise and disbelief, his face bulging with the soar of blood. Quickly he crossed to the mirror over the sink and thrust his face close.

'That damned razor,' he said.

He watched to see if I believed him, but now I saw other places.

'You cut your chin too, and your neck.'

'It's nothing.'

Nothing but lipstick. I felt shame and could not look at him. The lumber business. Partners. Father and son. I wanted to spew him, the sneak of him, the cheapness of him, the betrayal, the death in him, myself in him, my sister Clara and my brothers in him, all our days and nights, all our lives in him.

We didn't say anything as I gathered my books and papers. As I started to leave, he touched my shoulder but I jerked away into the dining room and then into my bedroom. In the snowy light that bounced through the window I undressed and slipped into bed beside my brother August. He jerked and said oh God as the liniment seared his nostrils.

The gleaming snow gave the room a phosphorescence. From the eaves above the window icicles hung like my mother's taffy, which had a way of congealing like patterns of jagged glass.

From the kitchen came a roaring sea of silence churned up by my father. Not that I cared, not one bit did I care. But I cared all the same. Why hadn't he wiped it off? Why had he been so careless and forced me to see it, the lip marks of some woman not my mother?

Those ugly dames at the Onyx! Where else in town could my father find another woman to kiss him? I saw them now, big-assed, hard-drinking women from the pottery factory, divorced women, married women who opened the saloon at ten in the morning and never left until it closed at two. It was a kind of exclusive club, a sorority of drinking women.

I could hear him in the kitchen, lathering soap, flooding his face with water, gasping and splashing like a man swimming for his life. His footsteps sounded and he came to the bedroom door.

'Come here,' he whispered.

'What for?'

'I want to talk to you.'

I got up in my shorts and followed him back to the kitchen. His face showed pain, his forehead wrinkled, his eyes pleading.

I waited in the doorway.

'Don't get the wrong idea,' he said. 'It's nothing. A crazy woman fooling around. I don't even know her name.'

'It's okay.'

'Sure it's okay. Just some crazy woman.'

I turned to go back to the bedroom.

'Wait a minute.'

I faced him again.

'You know how your mother is.'

'I won't say anything.'

'I get enough trouble. You understand?'

'Sure, Papa.'

'I don't care what you think of me, but don't hurt your mother.'

'I know.'

'You know what I'm saying?'

'I know.'

'Okay. Be a man.'

'Okay.'

I went back to the bedroom and lay down. The kitchen light went out and the floor creaked with his steps as he walked into the bedroom next to ours. There was a boom when his shoe hit the floor, and then another. I heard the tinkle of coins and nails as he pulled off his pants then the twang of bed springs as his weight descended at my mother's side.

I pictured them lying there in the darkness of different worlds, sharing the same manger, like a burro and a hen. Man and wife, side by side, in two nests of a sagging mattress, yet separated by the remains of their dead marriage. It had me writhing. Well, all right! So my mother wasn't much any more, with aching teeth that had to come out and hair streaked with grey that wouldn't stay in. She owned no rouge or lipstick, and her rear would look ridiculously small on one of those bar stools at the Onyx, but she would never leave the mark of her mouth on another man's face. She did what had to be done, submissive to the will of God – the laundry, the cleaning, the cooking, the raising of her family. All in all, it was enough to drive a man out of the house and you couldn't blame my father for running for his life. But those women! Those big-assed, loafing women! They knew he had a wife and family, yet they smeared their lipstick on him, and he was as bad as they for allowing it.

Sleep would not come as I twisted and groped, and my hand came upon something under August's pillow. I drew it carefully from under the weight of his head. It was a large brown envelope. For months I had been searching for that mysterious envelope, knowing he kept it hidden, his most secret possession.

He slept deeply with his mouth open and I sat up and drew out the contents of the envelope. They were glossy photographs of Carole Lombard, a varied collection, curiously luminous in that cold clear light. They showed her in bathing suits and evening gowns, in wide hats and pirate costumes, on horseback and in speed boats, on tiptoe in lingerie.

Then I found the real reason for August's secrecy. Some of the portraits were signed in his own handwriting. 'For my darling August, adoringly – Carole.' 'To August, with undying love – Carole.' 'For Augie, passionate memories of Malibu nights – Carole.' 'Dear August: do with me what you will. I am yours body and soul. Your Carole.'

You were supposed to laugh at such things, for they made you out a fool. I looked at him with his open mouth, his breath puffing steam into the frigid air. The autographs were not funny. He had written sad things, intimate things, too sacred for anyone else to see. He was fifteen, and I had got used to treating him as though he was no more than five or six. Yet there he was, only two years younger than myself, dreaming of Carole Lombard as fiercely as I dreamed of baseball. Tenderness filled me. I bent over and kissed his cold forehead. Then I put the pictures back into the envelope and slipped it under his pillow.

I lay there in the white night watching my breath escape in misty plumes. Dreamers, we were a house full of dreamers. Grandma dreamed of her home in faroff Abruzzi. My father dreamed of being free of debt and laying brick side by side with his son. My mother dreamed of her heavenly reward with a cheerful husband who didn't run away. My sister Clara dreamed of becoming a nun, and my little brother Frederick could hardly wait to grow up and become a cowboy. Closing my eyes I could hear the buzz of dreams through the house, and then I fell asleep.

Chapter Two

All at once I felt myself lifted awake out of the depth of sleep and feeling a presence close by. It was not a dream. Someone was in the bedroom besides my brother and myself. I opened my eyes.

The room was glacier cold, my breath funneling carbon monoxide into the frozen air. At the bedside stood a woman so near I could have reached out and touched her. Her gown was a flowing blue velvet, and her slender waist was cinched with a golden cord that matched her yellow hair. Her feet were in blue sandals with golden thongs. She looked down on me and smiled. For a moment I thought it was Carole Lombard. Her hand held a luminous globe, the planet earth, the land bodies in gold, the oceans and rivers a bright blue.

Suddenly it came to me who she was, and the shock pushed me trembling under the blankets. She was the Virgin Mary. She had to be. The bed trobbed with the beat of my heart and I was afraid to look again.

I shook my brother. 'Augie.'

'What?' He rolled away from me.

I shook him again and crawled closer.

'Somebody's here,' I whispered.

He bolted to a sitting position, suddenly wide awake and afraid. 'Where?' he said. 'I don't see anybody.'

I sat up and looked at the place where she had stood. She was gone. I pointed. 'She was right there. I saw her plain as day.'

'Who?'

'The Blessed Virgin.'

'Oh, shit!' he said, sinking back in disgust and pulling the covers over his head.

In the morning my mother woke us and I was troubled as I sat at the bedside and started dressing. Augie lay on his back, staring at the ceiling.

'Boy, did you have a nightmare.'

'It wasn't a nightmare. I saw her.'

'You're cracked.'

'I saw her, damn it!'

He kicked off the covers and pulled on his pants. 'Maybe you did, at that.' He bent over to put on his socks. 'She only appears for dimwits.'

'I tell you I saw her.'

'Do me a favor.'

'Not if I can help it.'

'Don't tell Mama. You know how she is. She'll believe you and make a shrine out of this room. She'll light candles and sprinkle holy water all over the place. We don't want to sleep in *no* grotto, like Lourdes.'

'Augie, I saw her. Honest to God.'

'I'm happy for you, Dom,' he smiled. 'I'm happy for the whole family. It isn't everybody that has a saint for a brother. No wonder we're so rich.'

We washed up and went to the kitchen for breakfast of oatmeal and coffee. Clara and Frederick were already there, finishing their meal. Grandma stood beside the table like a grim cop, holding tightly the two handles of the pewter sugar bowl. She was the self-appointed dispenser of sugar, opposed to its use in all forms, while we favored it in everything. Each morning she brought the sugar bowl from her bedroom, tightly clutching the handles with blue-veined hands, fighting us over every spoonful.

Clara and Frederick left for school, and Augie and I ate in silence while Mama sipped black coffee. Then Augie nudged me.

'Mama,' he said. 'You seen the Blessed Virgin lately?'

'Oh, yes,' she said, brightening.

'How was she?'

'Fine, fine. She's so lovely.'

'Was she in heaven?'

'Oh, no. She was in the chicken house.'

'Chicken house? Doing what?'

She leaned forward, her eyes widening with enthusiasm. 'She was kneeling at the foot of the cross, kissing our Lord's feet.'

Augie turned to me and nodded wisely.

'She have anything to say?'

'She said, "This is my beloved son, who died for the sins of the world."'

Augie grinned at me.

'Top that, jughead.'

'Shut up,' I said.

'I wish she'd call on *me* sometime,' he said. 'Some people have all the luck.'

'Just pray,' Mama said. 'Prayer brings all things.'

'You hear that, stupid? Pray!'

I scooped up a handful of oatmeal and shoved it into his face. He just sat there, the mush flaking from his nose and eyes, his smile unblemished.

'Oh, Dominic!' Mama said. 'Why?'

'Brother against brother,' Grandma groaned, her hands across her stomach. 'God help America!'

I grabbed my books and headed for school.

All morning the thing clung to me, a cobweb of remembering, too obstinate to brush aside. Had I really seen the Virgin Mary, or could it have been my mother standing at the bedside? It couldn't have been my mother. Had a strange woman drifted off the street and into our house? Perhaps it had been an optical illusion, a distortion of light and shadow. Who ever heard of a woman in blue velvet and gold sandals wandering into somebody's bedroom? And why did I sense her presence even before I saw her?

It began to get the best of me. I cut geometry and went for a walk. On the veranda of the rectory Father Murray paced back and forth in a black overcoat, reading his breviary. I started toward him to tell him of the vision and then I realized it wouldn't help at all, for he knew all the answers to all the dilemmas in heaven and on earth, and passed them around like so many sticks of gum.

I came to the side door of the church and stepped inside, smelling the incense of baptisms and funerals, of high mass and benedictions, the odor of myself, of my past life, of my life before I was born and after I died. My mother and father were married in this church, and we kids were baptized in it. Grandpa Giovanni's funeral took place here, as would Grandma's and the rest of us. In many ways it was like walking into the church of Torricella Peligna. I had never been there, but I knew it had to be very much like this, with the same essence of wax candles and frankincense, with a few old ladies kneeling in prayer the same as the two or three I now saw stooped before the Virgin's altar.

I dipped my finger in the holy water font, made the sign of the cross, and tiptoed across the slate floor to the Virgin's statue. Her waxen plaster face looked down as I went to my knees. She stood with bare feet crushing a serpent, the child Jesus in her arms. It was not an attractive statue, the Virgin's cheeks bloated, the jaw too square, the expression insolent rather than smiling. The infant had the face of a frowning old man, and he was not much larger than her hands.

I tried to pray. 'Was it you?' I asked. 'What does it mean?' I raised my eyes to her, and the more I stared the more ugly the statue became, until it came to me that I had not seen the Virgin at all, but an earthly creature, maybe Carole Lombard after all, or Garbo, or Jean Harlow, or Miriam Hopkins. My skull rattled with the confusion. It was meaningless and tiresome.

I was glad to hear the noon bell sounding, and when I stepped out into the schoolyard the sun was a horse ablaze in the sky, chasing a herd of clouds across the mountains. Boys clustered in little groups where the sunlight formed pools of warmth against the handball courts. In white middies and pleated skirts the girls gathered cackling about the nuns on the school steps, their voices like bursts of birds. Things were thawing out, the naked trees dripping, clumps of snow losing their grasp of the slate roof, sliding lazily to the rain gutters and plopping heavily on the ground.

I pushed myself up on the bike rail and felt the warm kiss

of the sun. What a day! I could almost see long fly balls and popups in the blue sky. Guys strolled past and paid their respects, asking about the old arm and saying it wouldn't be long now. When they said, 'Hi, Dom,' they were paying their respects to St Catherine's greatest pitcher, and not the kid with freckles and bunny ears.

Two freshmen strolled up, and one said, 'Hey, ain't you Dominic Molise?'

'Righto.'

It was like being interviewed by a couple of sports writers.

'I saw you pitch against Boulder Prep,' he said. 'Man, were you hot!'

I smiled modestly. 'A two-hitter, if memory serves.'

'You struck out nineteen.'

'One of my better days.'

'Hey, Dom. Do you use a spitter?'

I smiled mysteriously.

'The answer is, yes. But don't quote me.'

'Think we'll have a good team this year, Dom?'

'The pitching is in good hands.'

They grinned.

'How tall are you, Dom?'

'Around five seven.'

'Hell, I'm taller'n that.'

I just laughed. 'How are you with a bat in your hand, punk? And me throwing them?'

It stopped him cold. 'No hard feelings, Dom.'

'That's okay, Kid.'

They moved on.

Even The Arm began to stir, like a plant brought out into

the sun. I could feel it pulsing, coming out of hibernation, and I gave it a friendly squeeze. Easy, baby; it's still the middle of February, so don't let a flash of sunshine fool you; quiet down, go back to sleep. After school we'll toss a few, just enough to kick up a little blood.

Three o'clock that afternoon and it was snowing again, flakes as big as eucharist wafers, the sky in twilight darkness. It was four blocks to the Elks Club, where Ken Parrish and I worked out two or three times a week in the basement gym. Ken's father was grand exalted ruler of the Elks, and made arrangements for us to practice there. The gym was too small for batting practice, but we got a good workout standing at opposite ends of a single bowling alley and throwing the ball back and forth.

Ken wasn't there when I arrived. I put on a sweat suit and gym shoes and stretched out on a bench in the locker room, waiting for him. The basement windows were at the street level and I could see the snow falling on the sidewalk and the legs of passersby as they waded through the fresh storm.

It was a good time for me, the best part of my winter, these afternoons with Ken Parrish. He was a senior at Roper High, and my best friend. We kept alive from one day to the next just for baseball. Ken was back in Roper after being expelled from two Eastern prep schools, not for bad grades, but for ditching classes to watch the ball games at Fenway Park in Boston.

His idol was Lou Gehrig of the Yankees. He owned three broken Gehrig bats and a band-aid with Gehrig's dried blood and little hairs from Gehrig's thumb stuck to the adhesive. This is what happened: seated behind the Yankee dugout one afternoon, Kenny saw Lou Gehrig rip the adhesive from his thumb and toss it near the first base line. Racing down the aisle, Ken jumped over the barrier and down on the playing field, snatching the bandage off the grass as two ushers collared him. They marched him out of the park, but Ken had his souvenir and didn't mind.

After the game he hung around the Yankee dressing room until Gehrig came out. Ken asked the great man to autograph the bandage, and Lou did it with his own fountain pen. That blood-stained strip of tape now hung from the wall of Ken's bedroom, framed and under glass. He was sure that it would be worth a lot of money some day, but I had my doubts. Old ball-players fade away fast.

The Parrishes were the richest family in Roper. They owned the hardware store and the furniture company and lived in a three storey Tudor house up on College Hill. There was a tennis court on the grounds, and the only private swimming pool in town. They had three cars, a cook, a housekeeper and a fulltime gardener. Their lighted Christmas tree won first prize every year.

The massive brick house was like a castle built for one purpose, a fortress to protect their only daughter. Kenny often invited me there, so I knew Dorothy's bedroom was in the southwest corner on the second floor. Many a night in good weather and bad I went out of my way to walk past and glance up at her window. Sometimes I saw her up there, but usually not. Just seeing the light coming from the window, warm behind the curtains, made my heart speed up. I loved her. It was crazy, impossible and stupid, but I longed to be the rug she walked on, the bed she slept in, the soap that cleansed her skin, the toilet she sat on.

She was a senior English major at Colorado U., down at

Boulder, and a Kappa, and I had this endless yearning for her from the first time I saw her three years before, the summer she worked in her father's hardware store. My flesh shivers when I remember.

I had gone there that morning on an errand for my father, and she was behind the counter in a grey smock.

'Can I help you?' she said.

I told her I wanted to buy a Number Two mason's pencil.

'Is there really such a thing?' she smiled. 'I never heard of it.'

'Oh, sure,' I said. 'A big flat pencil.'

Her eyes were large and warm and grey, her hair in a trim bob, the friendliest blonde I ever saw. I knew who she was, for already she had fame as freshman queen at the university and at tennis, and her picture was often in the local paper and the *Denver Post*.

She asked her father where the pencils were and he pointed to a shelf near the front of the store. I followed her along a wall of merchandise shelves ten feet high. She walked like a cat, trim and fluid in white sneakers. Her smock was an inch shorter than the blue skirt beneath and her ass undulated with the snug compactness of an athlete's.

The pencils were up on a shelf near the ceiling and there was a tall ladder on a trolley which she moved into place. Without hesitation she started up the ladder.

'Wait,' I said. 'Let me.'

'Don't be ridiculous,' she smiled.

The ladder was perfectly safe, locked to guide rails above and below, but I held on to it with both hands, for no other reason than that you instinctively support a ladder when someone climbs it. I did something else without thinking, instinctively. I stared. What I saw I had never seen before in quite that fashion. Her rump, two loaves of round golden bread, a breath-taking cleavage between them, and a burst of hair like brass filings.

All my life I had brooded and pondered over the depressing unattractiveness of that place, having seen it beneath the dresses of my mother and my aunts, startling as a nest of mice, drab as the sweepings of a vacuum cleaner, obscene but obligatory, the harsh confrontation every man had to face some day. No wonder women kept it hidden. No wonder it was a sin to look at it, a sin to desire it, and an even greater sin to penetrate it unless you were married.

Yet there it was on the ladder five feet above me, a tawny cloud floating in the tent of her skirt, sunlight through the plate glass window striking it with electric perception, and I was hypnotized.

Then I heard her voice: 'That's the silliest expression I ever saw in my life.'

She was glaring down at me with a deadly smile. I felt shame and a flash of panic. I wanted to make a run for the street. She descended, and I kept my eyes away from her, backing off.

'Here you are.'

I turned to see her holding out the pencil, studying me not in anger but defiance.

'Ten cents,' she said.

I handed her a dime and took the pencil. Shaking and out of control, I turned to leave and crashed into a display of paint brushes on a wire rack. A few brushes hit the floor. I thought of running again. She stood looking at me.

I spluttered an apology and bent to pick the brushes up. 'I'll do that,' she said. 'Just go.'

I blundered out into the street. It was time to die, the end of my life. I walked down Twelfth Street, searching for a place where I could lie down and hide, never to rise again. After half a block I came to the alley. It was out of the sunlight and in shadow. I found a friendly garbage can and took hold of it with both hands, staring down at a turmoil of greasy rags, empty oil cans and chunks of machinery, longing to dive in and hide.

For weeks I thought of that morning, afraid to walk in front of the hardware store, thinking of it suddenly at odd times, having it explode in my memory like a bomb, holding my temples against it, ashamed to look at myself in mirrors, feeling it explode at night as I lay in bed writhing like a bullet had hit me. I blamed her, finally. She should not have gone up that ladder. She should have allowed me to go up. She had done it on purpose.

I never saw her again until her brother and I became friends and Kenny asked me over to his house. He took me into the Parrish living room and there she was – twenty-one now, beautiful as a glacier, her yellow hair down to her shoulders. She was sitting in a leather chair, reading through large, black-rimmed glasses. It had been three years since the fiasco in the hardware store, and I held my breath as we crossed the room and Kenny introduced me. She said, 'Hi,' over the top of her glasses and went back to the book on her lap. I breathed easier. She had not recognized me.

'Be right back,' Ken said. He dashed upstairs. I sat on the divan and we were more than alone together, because it was as if I wasn't even in the room. She sat near the window, the afternoon sun filtering through the gently swaying curtains. Her legs were under her, the silken knees glossy as golden globes. Even when she lit a cigarette her eyes ignored me, and I was glad.

The room was vast, with beam ceilings and a fire-place large enough to stand in. The chairs and divans were of soft green leather. Hundreds of books lined the walls. A phonograph played Ravel's *Bolero*, barely audible.

'Mind if I smoke?'

She picked up a pack of cigarettes and tossed it. I made a nice one-handed catch and said, 'Thanks, I got my own.'

More silence. I lit up and sat back in the comfortable chair, blowing smoke toward the beams.

'Sure have a lot of books,' I said.

Not a word. Her hand turned a page. I stood up and went over to the shelves. They were mostly new books, the kind displayed in the front window of Martin's Stationery Store: Hemingway, Caldwell, Bromfield, Waugh. My own reading range was strictly St Catherine style: *Quo Vadis*, *Life of St Teresa*, *Ivanhoe*, *The Deerslayer*, *Two Years before the Mast*.

Ken's mother was something else, plump and stylish, very social, always in the papers. She didn't like me, but she tried. Every time she came upon me in the house, her eyes flared in astonishment, and she had trouble remembering my name.

'Hello, Tony,' she'd say.

'Dominic. Dominic Molise.'

'And what is it Ken says you do so well?'

'Throw a baseball.'

'I see. Well, to each his own, I suppose.' And she'd turn to Kenny and say, 'Now I don't want you and Tony to get into any mischief.' Out she'd go to her car, driving off to some important meeting.

I didn't see much of Mr Parrish. He had been a great athlete at the university, but now he was grey and heavy, wearing the same tweed suit and chain-smoking cigarettes, worried about business, always listening to the news on the radio, hating Roosevelt, the Denver papers torn apart and strewn around his chair.

Kenny liked coming to my house. It was old and plain, but he was comfortable there, sitting beside the window in the kitchen, eating a dish of spaghetti or a bowl of minestrone with homemade bread. It pleased my mother to have him asking questions about her cooking. He was wild about Grandma Bettina, who buzzed him suspiciously, frowning at his handsome shoes, his tailored slacks and his cashmere sweaters. With folded arms she sat at the table and watched him eat, muttering insults in Italian that Kenny enjoyed but never understood.

'What's that?' he'd ask. 'What's she saying now?'

And I would translate, 'She says you're the son of a whore who's been banged from here to Palermo.'

'Marvelous!' he'd shout. 'Beautiful!' And he would leap from his chair and throw his arms around her, trying to kiss her as she slapped him with small hands and ran for her bedroom.

Waiting for Kenny, I half dozed on the locker room bench. The room was warm, smelling of steam and sweat and antiseptic. I could feel my future making waves around me, the promise of days to come, the exciting years that lay ahead. It was always this way with great men, a stirring in their bones, a mysterious energy that set them apart from the rest of mankind. They knew! They were different. Edison was deaf. Steinmetz was a hunchback. Babe Ruth was an orphan, Ty Cobb a poor Georgia boy. Giannini started with nothing. People thought Henry Ford was crazy. Carnegie was a runt like myself. Tony Canzoneri came out of the slums. Poor young men, touched with magic, lucky in America. Thank God my father had the good sense to leave Torricella Peligna! Times were bad, to be sure, with the depression going full strength, but what a glorious future lay ahead for those touched with fame.

Kenny arrived about four. He wore a fur hat and a three-quarter length sheepskin coat. It was brand new.

'Pretty nice,' I said, watching him peel it off.

'You want it?' He flung it to me. 'Take it. Be my guest.'

I told him, no thanks, for he did not mean it, a trick of his to make light of the fact that he had so much that was unimportant.

He felt lousy, kicking off his shoes and throwing them against the lockers.

'Fucking snow,' he said.

He pulled off his pants. He had his sister's features, the same grey eyes and bone structure. I was always surprised at his Dorothy legs, his lean Dorothy waist. His shorts were delicate and frivolous, the things one would expect to find on a girl, and I thought they foredoomed his future as a first baseman. No self-respecting ballplayer would dare show up in a locker room wearing shorts like that.

He put on his sweat suit and shoes, and we got our gloves and walked out to the bowling alley and began tossing the baseball, not talking, just warming up. Through the small windows we could see the snow falling heavily. It was depressing. One of my tosses was low and wild, under his glove, bouncing off the wall.

Disgusted, he didn't even turn to retrieve it.

'Screw it,' he said. 'Let's quit.'

'We barely started.'

He flipped his glove clear across the alley and into the locker room.

'It's madness. Two intelligent human beings tossing a baseball around in the Elks basement in a one-horse town in Colorado in the dead of winter. It's sickening.'

'It's better'n hanging around doing nothing.'

'I've had it, buster. I'm ready to blow this God-forsaken village. We're just jacking off.'

We stripped and showered. Under the stream of hot water I could see the snow falling outside. Roper was just a way-station on the road to the Hall of Fame. A man could bear up under any temporary crisis if he had faith in the future.

We dried off with the thick fluffy Elks Club towels. The street was dark now. We heard the clang of tire chains, the muted chimes of the courthouse clock striking five.

I stretched out on my back across the rubbing table and held up The Arm. 'He needs you, Ken. He's crying for your magic touch.'

'Okay, honey,' he said, patting the bicep.

Pouring alcohol into his palm, he smeared it over The Arm and began massaging it, starting at the finger tips and slowly working upward, kneading the alcohol into the pores, stroking and patting the muscles until the tension was gone and The Arm was soft and pliant, hanging limply in his grasp.

'Isn't he beautiful?' he said. 'Just like soft leather.'

I clinched my fist and felt the arm harden to iron all the way to the collarbone. It had never felt better. Here it was, only February, and The Arm was tuned up as if it was the middle of August.

He raised it by the finger tips and it was heavy and loose as a big fish. 'Priceless,' he said. 'A deadly weapon.'

I sat up, pleased.

'Thanks for taking such good care of him.'

'My pleasure, Dom. I envy you.'

'Don't. Nothing's happened – yet.'

'I'm just a half-assed high school ballplayer. I got no future at all.'

'Same here. My old man laid it out last night. He's gonna make a bricklayer out of me.'

'Over my dead body.'

'It's all worked out. I finish high school and start learning the trade.'

'He can't be that stupid! I'll talk to him.'

'He means well. He just doesn't understand, the poor dope.'

He grabbed me. 'Dom! Let's get out of here, before it's too late.'

'Where'll we go?'

'Catalina, where the Cubs are.'

'I thought you were a Yankee man.'

'They're in Florida. Too far, too late. Catalina's only fifteen hundred miles.'

'What'll we do when we get there?'

'Try out for the team, you ass.'

I got excited. 'You mean it?'

'As God is my judge!'

I jumped off the table and rubbed my hands together. I walked back and forth. I kicked a towel. 'Oh, God!' I said. 'Me with the Cubs!'

He danced up and down, his balls bouncing. He crossed to his locker and got out a pack of cigarettes. We lit up. After a couple of drags we grew calm, thoughtful.

'I want to ask you something,' he said.

'Shoot.'

'In strict confidence. The truth.'

'Okay.'

'Don't lie to me, Dom. Oh God, don't deceive me! It's too important.'

I covered my heart.

'You have my word of honor.'

He hesitated, ground out his cigarette. 'Am I good enough to try out for the Chicago Cubs?'

Pow! What a question! His hungering eyes begged for only one answer. Any other would have been a knife through his heart. Also, the end of our friendship. I had to play it out, make it good. I crossed to the locker and pulled on my shorts, then moved to the mirror and combed my hair.

'You're destroying me, Dom.'

'You've got to give me a little time to think this out,' I told him. 'I hate to say anything that will change the course of your life. It's a tough question. I wish to God you hadn't asked me.'

A sickly smile turned his lips.

'You don't have to answer. I already know what you're going to say.' He leaned forward, elbows on his knees, and covered his face.

'Don't jump to conclusions, Ken. I'm still thinking.'

'Go ahead and say it. Tell me I'm nothing but a bush leaguer.' He laughed, a cackling, insincere laugh, and then spoke bitterly. 'You could be wrong, you know! I'm still young, still developing, I got great hands, I hit a long ball. Hell, I got just as good a chance as you!'

I walked over to him and laid my palms on his shoulders and smiled. 'Kenny, you asked me a question. I haven't answered it yet.'

'Then answer, for God's sake! Stop torturing me!'

'Ken Parrish, you're the finest first base prospect I ever saw. Right now, as a fielder, I'd say you're major league caliber. In three, four years you'll surpass Charlie Grimm, maybe your idol Lou Gehrig. As for hitting, how can I ever forget your three homers against Fort Collins? One of them musta gone four hundred feet. Ken Parrish, you're ready! You're a major leaguer right now, right this moment.'

A big sigh and he held out his hand.

'Thanks, Dago.'

We shook hands.

'I had to be honest,' I said. 'At the same time, I didn't want it to go to your head.'

'I appreciate your frankness.'

Now it was my turn.

'I'd like to ask *you* a question.'

'Fire away, pal.'

'I was honest with you. Now I want you to be honest with me.'

'That's what friends are for. What's on your mind, Dom?'

'The same thing: what are my chances with the Chicago Cubs?'

He frowned. 'Pheew, that's a tough one.'

'Not if you're my friend, it isn't.'

'I'll have to think it over.'

'Go ahead, take your time.'

He squeezed his chin and lapsed into silence. I watched him slip into his shorts and shirt, then his pants. He was concentrating, squinting at the ceiling. He put on his socks and shoes, crossed to the mirror, and fastened his necktie. Then he wet and combed his hair. If he was trying to irritate me it wasn't working, because I already knew the answer. Still, he was taking a long time, longer than I did.

'Well?' I said.

'Just one thing bothers me. How tall are you?'

'What's that got to do with it?'

'Let's face it,' he shrugged. 'Good pitchers are tall, rangy.'

I didn't care for that.

'How tall are you, Parrish?'

'Six feet.'

I folded my arms and circled him. 'And you call yourself a good hitter?'

'The best,' he grinned. 'You said so yourself.'

'How many hits you had off me in the last three years?'

'I've had my share,' he said, being very gay about it. 'Five or six, maybe.'

'You're a dirty fucking liar! You've only had one hit off me, and that was a lucky single when you fell away from a pitch and blooped it into right field!' I pushed up close to him, my shoulder in his chest. 'You know how I pitch to you, Parrish? In tight, close to your cock, because you haven't got the guts to stay in there and swing!'

I bulled him against the wall.

'Wait a minute!' he said, holding me at arm's length. 'You asked me a question: do I think you're ready for the Cubs. Do you want to hear my answer or not?'

'No, I don't.'

He shrugged. 'Suit yourself.'

We grew silent. The steam pipes hissed. I gathered up my stuff and slammed it into a pile in the locker. He pulled on his new coat and adjusted his fur hat before the mirror. Then he turned to leave. I didn't want it to end that way. We had too much going for each other, too many good times in the past.

'Wait a minute,' I said.

He stopped, came back.

'I'm not mad at anything,' I said.

'Why should you be?' he smiled. 'You're the greatest left hand prospect in America today.'

'Why didn't you say so in the first place?'

'I was testing you. The mark of a great pitcher is desire. And confidence. You've got it, Dom.'

I held out my hand.

'Thanks, Ken.'

We shook hands. He clung to my fingers, turned my hand over. 'The fingers of an artist,' he said. 'Just as precious as Yehudi Menuhin's. When I think of them laying brick it makes my blood run cold.'

I stared at my ten fingers, thick and short and powerful, like my father's must have been before falling brick and mason's tools twisted them like root stumps, like the claws of a bear. It made me writhe. I kicked the lockers.

'I'll *never* lay brick!' I swore. 'May God strike me dead if I ever pick up a trowel.'

'Catalina!' Ken gasped. 'Palm trees along the blue Pacific! Blue skies bathed in sunlight, warm tropic nights! No snow! A little island paradise where all you do is play baseball and eat good food in a fine hotel.'

'I'm listening.'

'Think of it! And here we are, down in this ratty old basement, buried alive in a snowstorm. My God, Dominic! Catalina's just over the mountains, a measly fifteen hundred miles away!'

It burst out of me: 'Let's go, Kenny! Let's get the hell out of here before we die!'

'Shake on it.'

We shook hands again.

'When?'

'Tomorrow,' he said. 'We'll grab a bus and be there in two days.'

That cooled me off. There were problems.

'How much will it cost?'

He figured fifty apiece, until we signed our contracts. I groaned. All the furniture in our house, including the kitchen stove, wasn't worth that. I remembered my father's slack jaw as he counted off our debts – the rent, the lights, the milk man, the grocery store, the coal company, the doctor, the lumber yard. We were so broke that even the poor nuns at St Catherine's accepted us tuition free.

And there was Kenny in his new coat and English shoes and fur hat, talking of fifty dollars as if it was fifty cents, and I screamed out, and what I said was:

'Why doesn't your sister Dorothy ever talk to me? What's she so snobby about? What did I ever do to her? What am I, a bum or something? She turns her back every time she sees me. It's insulting!'

His jaw hung open in amazement.

'What's Dorothy got to do with this?'

'Plenty!' I said, buzzing around, kicking the wet towels, slamming lockers shut. 'Plenty, that's all. You don't think so? You want to stick up for her? Okay. So screw you, and your big-assed mother and your grouchy old man, and your big house and your servants and your cars and your money.'

There was a silence and I was sick and ashamed and frightened that it had spewed out of me like a mad dog.

He sat down, folded his hands, and stared at the floor. 'Well, I'll be damned,' he said. Then he shrank from me, going farther and farther away, and I spat in shame. What a vile thing to have burst from me, like pus from a blister. Dorothy Parrish had always been such a secret thing, quiet and filling me with sweet longing, a lovely girl in a chair reading a book on a summer afternoon with the sun in her hair, a dream.

Nothing was left between us now. Even Catalina wasn't worth the effort. We were strangers. Maybe our friendship was over, maybe we were enemies. As we climbed the stairs into the darkness of the street I was certain we had had our last workout in the Elks gym.

The snow fell so heavily we couldn't see the courthouse across the way. Cars moved bleakly in the mournful traffic, headlights dim and shrouded. We plodded a block to the bus stop on Pearl Street, beside the snow-bloated popcorn wagon. Usually I waited until the bus picked him up and we talked of when we would meet again. Now he drifted away to stand alone against the wall of the bank, hands in the pockets of his sheep-skin coat, peering up the street for the approach of his bus, snowflakes powdering his coat. Finally the white eyes of the bus came out of the gloom. He moved up to the curb.

'Well,' he smiled. 'Cool off, Dago.'

It made me furious. I grabbed his throat.

'Don't ever call me that again!'

His eyes popped in astonishment. I let go and he turned and entered the bus. It drew away, spewing the smell of oil as it vanished into the storm. I shoved my hands into my pockets and started up Pearl Street, slogging home in the slush of the pointless storm. But the snow had its consolations after all. It hid you from others, your freckles and fan-shaped ears and miserable stature, and you drifted past other ghosts in the desolation, heads bent, eyes hidden, your guilt and worthlessness deep and protected inside.

Chapter Three

Supper was ready, the table set in the dining room. We waited, Grandma watching at the front window.

'He'll come,' Mama said. 'He knows we're having lamb.'

She looked almost festive, her hair braided and in a pile, wearing a fresh house dress, a fragrance of lilacs following her – too much talcum powder.

By seven we knew he would not come, and we sat down to minestrone, breast of lamb stuffed with rice and raisins, peppers in garlic and olive oil, and jello.

Mama wouldn't eat. She left the table and we heard her in the kitchen, washing pots and pans. Two empty places at the table now, the wine carafe beside Papa's napkin.

'I'd call the police,' Clara said.

'What for?'

'Teach him a lesson.'

She had always been Mama's loyal ally. She was now thirteen, suddenly sassy and hostile, longing for her own bedroom instead of sharing the front room with Frederick, sleeping on the unyielding leather sofa.

'Hanging around that dirty old poolhall!' she said. 'I wouldn't let *my* husband get away with it.'

'Be quiet,' I said, brooding about Kenny, knowing I had lost my best friend.

'I won't be quiet. What do you know? You're a man, like your father. That's the way it always is, the men against the women.'

'What can you expect from America?' Grandma growled. 'Cards and poolhalls, whiskey and women! Give me the sweet poverty of Christ and the good old days. At least the towns were small and a man could not wander far, and came home when he was hungry.'

We carried our dishes into the kitchen and started homework while Clara and Mama did the dishes. Many times my father was away from home, but tonight something was wrong. It was in the air we breathed.

'Don't, Mama,' Clara said, and we glanced from our books to see our mother crying softly. She dried her red hands and ran through the dining room to her bedroom.

Clara finished the dishes and brought her books to the table. We were miserable and it was hard to concentrate. We couldn't hear Mama crying, but even the house was aware of her tears, the floors her feet had trod, the pieces of furniture, the friendly old stove, the pots and pans, the dish towel by the sink, still wet from her hands.

'Go to your mother,' Grandma said.

She lay with her head on the pillow, looking at the ceiling, her eyes like wet birds. I sat at the bedside and took her cold, weightless hand and asked if there was something I could do.

'He lied,' she said bitterly. 'He always lied. And now it's too late.'

She sat up and blew her nose.

Across the room, under the dresser, were my father's work shoes, not worn for months, gnarled and misshapen and chalk white from mortar, the toes turned up like the shoes of a dead man.

'I don't blame him anymore,' she said, looking at herself in the mirror. 'I'm old, I'm nothing, I never was. No wonder I married him! There wasn't anybody else.'

'You look just fine, just right.'

It was the best I could say, and it was true. I would not have wanted her any other way. She was not a beauty, but she was beautiful, a mater dolorosa, like the mother of God.

Holy pictures stared down at us from the walls, the madonna over the bedside, the Savior with his exposed and bleeding heart above the headboard, a statue of St Anthony on the dresser, St Teresa across the room. It was like a nun's cell, and I wondered again how they could make love in a room like that, yet all four of us had been conceived there, on that very bed.

'He never cared for me,' she said bitterly. 'He really wanted to marry your Aunt Flora, but she couldn't stand him. When he gave her the ring she wouldn't have it on her finger, she threw it in the sink and laughed, and then he gave it to me to spite her. And that's how I married your father.'

'Didn't you love him?'

'I felt sorry for him, if that's what you mean.'

I couldn't bear the curled up shoes under the dresser, pale and luminous and grotesque. I rose from the bed and dropped them with a boom in the closet.

'He likes them under the dresser,' she said.

'They give me the creeps.'

'So we got married, and he told me about our wonderful house in Roper. My own house!' It made her smile to remember it. 'You don't know what that means to a woman.

In the forest, he said, right by a little stream, a place to raise children. We took the train from Denver, and he said he lost the tickets, and the conductor waited and waited, and then he said he lost his wallet too. I felt so sorry for him because he had that funny Italian accent and the conductor didn't understand a word, so I paid the fare myself. Somebody rob me, he said, somebody steal nine hundred dollars. The poor man. He married me without a penny, not even a dollar to give the priest.'

She kept glancing at the vacant place where the shoes had been, and now she rose from the bed, crossed to the closet, lifted out the ghostly shoes, and placed them under the dresser once more. In the mirror she studied the tumble of disarrayed hair and began removing hairpins, holding them in her mouth, speaking through them:

'And then I saw my house, my wonderful house in the forest.' Her eyes took in the bedroom, her smile touched with irony. 'You think this house is cold and worn out? You should have seen that place on Roper Creek! A shack near the old city dump. Made of old lumber and tin roofing. No water, no sink, no toilet. We had to go out under the trees. And the furniture – boxes to sit on, a mattress for a bed, an oil drum for a stove. Oh God, how he lied to me!'

Her hair tumbled over her shoulders and she ran her fingers through it and cried. 'Then that old lady in the next shack came over and knocked on the door and said could she have her furniture back, because he'd borrowed it – the boxes, the stove, the mattress, and I helped her carry it out, and there wasn't anything left, just the dirt floor.'

I thought how terrible it must have been for her, but I

pitied my father too. She had only been the victim, while he had been both the victim and the betrayer.

'Poor guy,' I said.

'He lied!' she shot back.

'He was poor, trapped.'

'He was a liar.'

'He was proud, so he lied.'

'How can a liar have pride?' She went to the window where the glass had frosted. Shuddering, she held her elbows and turned away. 'I don't blame your father anymore. I blame myself. If you put up with a man's lies, you're as bad as he is. You're a liar, same as him.'

A horn sounded in the street. By the time I got to the front door Clara and my brothers were already there, looking at a grey sedan parked at the curb. It had to be Kenny in his Dad's car.

'Wow!' Augie said. 'A brand new LaSalle. Look at that long snazzy hood!'

I ran out in my shirt sleeves. Kenny was behind the wheel, and at his side was the unbelievable, beautiful Dorothy. She was in a mink coat with a white scarf around her neck, her honey hair inside the deep collar. She was smiling, actually looking into my face and meeting my eyes for the first time. I felt myself floating, coming off the ground, and I had to grab the car to keep myself down, stunned and without words.

'Hi,' she smiled.

It was more eloquent than all of Tennyson. My God, what a lovely thing to say! My God, how inspiring, how moving! How clever she was!

'Hi,' I answered, but even then I was afraid I had said too

much, a long speech that bored her. Kenny was watching me. He laughed.

'Get your coat, Dom.'

'Sure. What for?'

'A Ginger Rogers picture at the Apollo. She wants to see it.'

Was it really happening? Was I making the whole thing up? Had I gone stark raving mad and run out into the street, imagining the whole thing? I stared at the sparkling face before me, the wide-set grey eyes, the ravishing mouth out of which cunning white vapors appeared.

'Please come,' the mouth said.

Beautiful. Better than Shakespeare. I almost went under. Her fragrant perfume wafted from within the car and enveloped me like a pink cloud, and I went staggering back to the house in a gurgle of enchantment, without feet, a zephyr, a floating thing pushed along by the motor of my heart.

'Who are they?' Grandma said. 'What do they want?'

'It's Kenny,' I said, pushing past them.

'The hottest car on the road today,' Augie said.

'It looks like a hearse,' Bettina said. 'Where are they taking you, to the graveyard?'

I shoved them away from the door and closed it. 'Animals,' I said.

While I changed shirts, Augie brought me his mackinaw, the best thing he owned. I tried to comb my hair at the mirror but I trembled so much I couldn't part it straight, and gradually I began to conk out, couldn't even think of being so near her, sharing the same car seat with her, and a numbing futility came over me. I sank on the bed, my hands dangling between my knees as I felt myself turning into an ox or some thick four-legged beast. I could almost feel my ears growing larger, and animal hair growing on my face. What was the use? No matter what the night held, I knew I would blow it sky high. What could I say when those cool grey eyes measured me? What if she kissed me? I would drop dead.

From the street the LaSalle horn blared sharply. Frederick raced into the room.

'Hurry up! They're waiting!'

'I don't feel so good.'

Augie shook me and pulled me to my feet. He snatched the bottle of Sloan's from the dresser and twisted off the cork.

'Here. Use it.'

'I'll stink.'

'Just breathe it, till you get your strength back.'

He shoved the bottle under my nose and I inhaled from my knees. It helped. My bones were hardening up, my muscles tightening, the pungency enveloping me like a hot flame, until I stood straight and courageous, tears running from my eyes as the liniment curled the hairs in my nostrils.

Then I remembered who I was – not some crumb bum nobody, but The Arm, the can-do man, the must-be man, the got-it man, not the hey-kid man, but the man with the bucket of sliders, the clutch man, Mister Hall of Fame.

Augie held the mackinaw up and I slipped into it, calm restored. I sauntered into the front room, past the crowd at the front door, and out to the waiting car. The front door opened and I slipped into the seat beside the dream. Ken touched the starter. There was a crunch of ice as the car moved into the street.

The miracle. All my hours of longing for her, all the aimless impossible reveries, and suddenly she was beside me golden and holy. The car was warm and cozy and I exulted in the intoxication of her perfume. She moved slightly, an accidental pleasure of her knee against mine. Like a kiss. What would happen next was unfathomable, beyond imagination. She might even speak to me.

The snow was deep over the iced pavement and Ken drove carefully, twenty miles an hour. The elms along Arapahoe were laced with snow. The street lights gave the snow a glittering warmth, sensuous white mounds like loaves of bread. Not a soul walked the streets, and only an occasional car passed, floating by as if in slow motion.

We turned off Arapahoe and moved north up Twelfth Street toward downtown. She had not spoken a word and seemed content to gaze ahead at the oncoming street. She lit a cigarette with the dash lighter and a lazy bubble of enchanting smoke tumbled from the intimate warmth of her mouth. Her smoke. Different. Overpowering.

Kenny spoke to her. 'Remember now, you promised to behave.' To me he said, 'I told her what you said this afternoon.'

The fool. It had me embarrassed.

'You talk too much,' I said.

Her hand took mine.

'I agree,' she said.

I felt the smooth warmth of her black kid glove squeezing my hand. 'I'm sorry if I was rude,' she added. 'It's just that all you and Ken talk about is baseball.'

'Don't you like baseball?'

'I can live without it.'

'What *do* you like?'

'Tennis, skiing, books. I love James Joyce.'

'You mean Jim Joyce, short stop for the St. Louis Browns?'

'Oh, my God.'

She exhaled, impatiently snuffed out her cigarette. Kenny grinned.

'She means Joyce, the writer.'

Me and my big mouth. I had never heard of him. She grew rigid, folding her arms and staring straight ahead.

'Oh, *that* one!' I said, trying to cover my ignorance, but it was useless and I knew she was convinced that I was a boob. I looked at her face, her jaw hard, her teeth clamped. I wanted to jump out and roll under the wheels of the car. She refused to speak another word.

'See what you've been missing?' Ken said. 'A pure unadulterated bitch.'

He wheeled into the curb across the street from the Apollo. I stepped out fast, almost in flight, then remembered to offer her my hand to help her down, but she ignored it and swept past me, bundling her fur around herself and hurrying toward the theatre, Ken following her.

I stood there with iced blood, feeling sick and unable to move. The iron fence around the courthouse was only a few feet away, and beyond it a growth of snow-laden lilac bushes. I thought of leaping the fence and walking away, clear to Wyoming. I was in the wrong state, with the wrong girl, afraid of her, afraid to breathe in her presence. But there was still another way out. I could rush down to the railroad track and throw myself in front of the eight o'clock local from Greeley, hurl myself at the cow-catcher, crushed chest, split skull, blood all over, Roper youth commits suicide, parents identify body of Dominic Molise, well-known athlete.

'Hey, come on!'

Kenny was waving in front of the theatre. I crossed the street. Dorothy stood under the marquee, stamping her shoes. I had no money of course and Kenny bought the tickets. She glanced at me fleetingly, cold as a star, as Kenny stepped away from the ticket booth and we went inside.

The place was almost empty, maybe twenty people. A newsreel was showing former President Hoover playing golf. Half a dozen patrons booed. We sat in the back loges where smoking was allowed, Dorothy between us. She flung back her fur and I tried to help her with it, but she did it herself, crisply, wanting no help from me. A dizzying fragrance filled the air, released by the open coat. I drew it in and heaved a sigh. She put a cigarette to her lips and waited for a light from either of us. Like mad I went scavenging through my pockets, and I was still pawing as Ken lit her Camel. She exhaled and sat back, waiting for the newsreel to end.

Then the first of two features hit the screen. It was Tom Mix in *The Man From Nogales*.

'Oh, shit,' she whispered, knowing she would have to sit through it until Ginger Rogers appeared in *Dancing Daughters*.

The western bothered her from the first shot of Tom Mix and Tony. For ten minutes she fussed restlessly, crossing and uncrossing her legs as the screen blazed with gunfire.

Suddenly she said, 'I can't stand it,' gathered up her coat and stalked up the aisle. I turned in surprise and watched her leave the theatre.

'What happened?'

Ken slouched deeper into his seat.

'She doesn't like cowboy pictures.'

'Maybe we better go too.'

'Not me. I love Tom Mix.'

I rose and hurried up the aisle. When I reached the street she was slipping behind the wheel of the LaSalle. I called to her and she saw me and started the engine. I ran across the street as the car began to move, crunching snow.

'Wait.'

The car stopped and the grey eyes, almost solemn now, turned to me.

'What is it?'

'Don't go. Stay.'

She flexed her shoulder.

'It's so childish, all that shooting.'

The night wind tossed her hair, fluttered her white scarf against her black gloves. Her breath fluted out like a flower in the cold air. I could have stared forever.

'It's so cold,' she shuddered. 'Why don't you go back with Ken and enjoy the show?'

But I couldn't leave her. I might never be alone with her again. A man got such few chances with a girl like her.

'I have to talk to you,' I said. 'It's very important.'

'Some other time.'

'I'm desperate, Dorothy. Help me. I need your advice. I need it bad.'

Her eyebrows lifted.

'Desperate?' She was amused. 'How can I possibly give you any advice?'

'I know you can.'

'How, for heaven's sake?'

'By just listening. You're a psychology major, aren't you?'

She considered it carefully.

'Get in,' she said without enthusiasm.

I ran around to the other side and sat beside her. She shifted gears and the car crawled into the street. At last we were alone, Dorothy Parrish and Dominic Molise. It was the high point of my life.

She drove slowly, without speaking, as if to give me time to gather my thoughts. I knew I had to be good, and I went rummaging through my mind, trying to find something of value. Then it came to me, the vision of the virgin standing at my bedside.

We drove up Pearl Street. The store windows were lit but the street was deserted. To the west a cumulus cloud sat like a swan on Flagstaff Mountain. She turned on Walnut and we went past the Onyx with its blazing neon lights. People sat along the bar, and juke box music spilled into the street.

'Well, young man. What's your problem?'

'A dream I had. It worries me.'

Her eyes turned to me and they were troubled and uneasy.

'Maybe I'm not the person to talk to. Dreams are so personal. Shouldn't you see a psychiatrist?'

'It's not that bad. I mean, it's not sinful or anything like that.'

'Are you sure?'

'Sure I'm sure. It's got the Virgin Mary in it.'

'I don't know a thing about her. Why don't you talk to the priest?'

I told her about the mysterious visitation, how I had wakened Augie, who failed to see it. As I talked we cruised up and down the town, out to the picnic grounds, up to the Chautauqua, around the junior college campus, the car very warm from the humming heater under the dash-board.

When she slipped her arms out of her fur coat I helped her, and she thanked me as it fell away from her, a nest of mink lined with golden silk. Beneath was a white turtleneck sweater and a green wool skirt, and knees round and smooth.

Even as I talked, I dared not look at her too closely. Every detail sent a small explosion through me – the curve of her elbow, the chiseled perfection of her nostrils, the heavy languor of her hair, the jeweled perfection of her wristwatch, the lipstick on her cigarette, her in-curving belly, the smoothness of her lap, her jaunty breasts sailing gaily ahead of the rest of her, bouncing with vitality.

The visitation baffled and fascinated her, but she insisted that it was nothing more than a dream. The luscious words of her mouth spilled out like globules of music, and I put every syllable carefully away in the storehouse of my mind, swearing to remember them forever. How beautiful Roper was now! How near the lovely mountains! What enchanting streets, what dear people in quiet chimneys! How fortunate to be alive, how exciting the future!

All of it, the incredible of it, the perfection of that moment, pounded around my waist and thighs, booming like a drum stretched tight, painful, writhing, the delicious torment spreading through me.

She had studied dreams, she said, herself never imagining what was happening inside of me. 'A dream is like a baseball. You have to remove the horsehide and unravel all the string before you get to the core.'

'That's fine,' I told her. 'Let's do that. Let's unravel it.'

'It will take time.' She glanced at me, smiling. 'Do you mind?'

'Oh, no. Take all the time you want. You've helped a lot. I don't know how to thank you. I'm learning things I never knew before. You make everything so clear.'

She was pleased.

'How about a cup of coffee?'

'It keeps me awake,' I said, knowing I didn't have a penny.

'If we're going to discuss this, you'll *have* to keep awake. We could have it at my house.'

'Good idea.'

We were clear over on the south side of town, touring around the bandstand at the fair grounds. She made the circle and we started back toward the center of town. The drum at my loins stretched tighter, waves of pain spreading across my back and down my legs. I had a hard-on like a quivering spear, a serious problem, and I knew it. When we reached her house and she saw me standing in the light our discussion would end right there.

I asked, 'Would you mind stopping at the Elks? I left a book down in the gym.'

'Not at all.'

We were back downtown again.

'How old are you?' she asked.

'Old enough. Age isn't important.'

'Seventeen is important. You're seventeen, aren't you?'

'Almost eighteen.'

She pulled up alongside the curbing at the Elks Club.

'Since we're asking, how old are you?'

'Twenty-three.'

'That's not too old.'

'Too old for what?'

'I mean, you're not an old woman.'

She smiled. 'Too old for you.'

I said nothing, but I didn't agree. She could have been seventy and it would not have mattered. When she was eighty I would be seventy-four, and when she got to a hundred I would be ninety-four, so what the hell difference did age make?

I stepped from the car, my loins shrieking help murder as I stood erect and felt a tightening of bolts and nuts. But my brother's mackinaw covered me to the knees as I walked without flinching down the snowy steps to the gym.

The basement was dark and very warm from overhead steam pipes. I crossed to my locker, pulled off my pants, and slipped into a jockey strap. Then I got into my pants again and stood before the mirror. The jock did its job, concealing everything that might be embarrassing. There was nothing new in this technique. Many people used it.

When I got back to the car, she saw that I was empty-handed. 'Couldn't find it,' I said.

We drove to the Parrish house and she brought the car into the garage beside her mother's Buick. Carrying her coat, I followed her up the stairs of the service porch. She opened the door and flipped on the light. We were in the kitchen.

A great room. White enamel stove and refrigerator, all manner of copper pots and pans hanging from the low beams, a floor of shining red tiles. The breakfast nook was a large oak table surrounded by captains' chairs. At the center sat a bowl of apples and oranges.

She took the fur from me, flung it over the back of a chair, and told me to make myself at home. I took off the mackinaw and sat down, watching her move back and forth across the gleaming floor as she prepared the coffee.

'Suppose we start at the beginning,' she said. 'Tell me what happened again.'

I talked and ate her with my eyes. Her pretty ass beneath the green skirt was as firm as a basketball. What grace she had. She made coffee-brewing a ballet. I never knew that opening a cupboard could be so beautiful. When she brought the cream pitcher to the table and set it down, the pressure inside the jock mounted like a time-bomb.

'Are you hungry?' she asked.

'I don't mind.'

'How about scrambled eggs?'

'Fine. Can I help?'

'If you like.'

I glanced at my hands. They could do with soap and water. She nodded toward a door. 'The bathroom's through there.'

The door opened to a laundry room, the bathroom at the other end. I washed and dried my hands and started back to the kitchen. A clothesline running the length of the laundry room caught my attention. It was strung with a dozen panties hanging there like a crowd of laughing girls. Some were blue, some pink, some were white and some were gold. They were too exquisitely small to belong to Mrs Parrish. They could adorn none but the glory of my life, the sacred silks of my beloved. Hot damn! I was getting my fill of her tonight! I walked along the line and let my face brush each pair. They stroked my nostrils, they ruffled my hair. Twelve there were. So many, and I had none, not one for a trophy to take away for remembrance sake. The gold one beckoned my eye. It had black sequins around the edges, feather soft, sweet as an oriole. One for me, eleven for Dorothy; it was more than fair. I unhooked the clothespins and stuffed it under my shirt. I felt it close to my flesh, breathing there, cuddled happily.

Then I walked into the kitchen. Dorothy was at the sideboard, breaking eggs and spilling them into a bowl. Just watching the oval things crack in her white fingers and spill forth with a golden plop created a series of small explosions inside me. My calves shuddered as she scrambled them with a fork and they turned yellow like her hair. She poured a bit of cream into the mixture and the silken smoothness of the descending cream had me reeling. I wanted to say, 'Dorothy Parrish, I love you,' to take her in my arms, to lift the bowl of scrambled eggs above our heads and pour it over our bodies, to roll on the red tiles with her, smeared with the conquest of eggs, squirming and slithering in the yellow of love.

I made the toast and she buttered it while we talked of deathless matters, like the weather, the movies, and the fact that everybody had a cold. We went to the round table and ate the eggs and toast and drank the coffee.

She ate ravenously, excitingly, and I envied every morsel that passed her lips. I listened to her teeth grinding toast, I heard a gulp when she swallowed coffee, and I thought I detected an enchanting gurgle somewhere in her lovely intestines, a limpid whimper, a note of pure music.

She got nowhere with the vision, and I knew she was trying to extract elements it did not contain. She showed off a bit too, with words like libido and the id. When my fingernails caught her eye she lifted my hand to study the thick stubbed nails.

'How long have you been biting them?'

'All my life.'

'Don't worry about it. The new theory about nail-biting is that it's just a harmless tensional outlet. I agree with Voellerts. It's probably good for you.'

'Fine, fine. I've been worrying about it for years. I feel a lot better now.'

That pleased her. 'Now then, let's get to the root of the matter. Your father. How do you get along with him?'

'Okay. We manage.'

'Do I detect hostility in that?'

'We have our disagreements.'

She smiled confidently. 'I thought so. You really hate him, don't you?'

'I feel sorry for him.'

'Pity?'

'He's out of work, with a big family to support. Why shouldn't I?'

She lit a cigarette and zeroed in: 'Pity, you know, is a form of superiority. I think you enjoy seeing him suffer.'

'I don't think so.'

She pursued it hotly. 'You hate your father because you resent his attentions toward your mother.'

'Trouble is, he doesn't pay any attention at all.'

'Trouble?' She jumped at this. 'You say "the trouble?" Why?'

'My mother's a plain woman. I think he's tired of her.'

'Now I see it all,' she said triumphantly. 'That wasn't the Virgin. It was your mother.'

'Couldn't have been. My mother has dark hair, and the Virgin was a lot younger.'

'Don't you see? The Virgin was the woman you *want* your mother to be!'

Her eyes were big and luminous. I could see myself reflected in the pupils, convexed, my face, my eyes, the fruit bowl.

'I'm so happy,' she sighed. 'I'm helping you. I honestly feel I'm making a contribution.' She put her hand on mine. 'What's your brother like? How do you feel about him? Do you quarrel?'

'A lot.'

'About what?'

'Everything.'

She rose in excitement and began to pace. 'That's interesting. Very interesting!' She paced with her golden mane bobbing, swinging about to face me, her arms flung wide, her chest bursting:

'I have it! Sibling rivalry!'

She leaped at me and put her two hands on my shoulders, her wet lips spilling over with excitement.

'You're jealous of your brother because your mother loves him more than she loves you! It's true, isn't it?'

'No.'

She groaned. 'You're not cooperating. You have to be honest, or we're wasting time.'

'I'm trying.'

She shook me.

'Think hard, Dominic. Go back to your early childhood. Far, far back to your earliest memories. What kind of toilet training did you have?'

'You're on the wrong track now.'

'Am I?' She was full of assurance. 'Think back. Was it a problem?'

I could only think of now, that moment of being with

her, not of potty time and peeing the bed ages ago. 'I don't remember,' I said.

'It doesn't surprise me. A case of adolescent amnesia: the unconscious compulsion to forget unpleasant facts. We all have it. More coffee?'

She crossed to the stove, gliding like a golden snake, and I stared and hungered and felt a demon rising in me, a surging urgency, nothing ventured nothing gained, now or never, do or die.

'I love you,' I said.

She put down the coffee pot and turned around thoughtfully, amused and not amused, not quite believing.

'Don't be silly,' she smiled.

'I love you.'

Now or never. I stood up without feet and found myself pulled toward her, falling to my knees before her, my arms around her hips, my face in the depths of her dress, and the demon had me totally in his power.

'I love you, I love you!'

'Stop it!'

She writhed and fought to free herself.

'Let go of me, you idiot!'

But the demon gave me strength and I pressed kisses against her belly and thighs as she struggled to break away. Then her feet went out from under her on the shining tiles and she fell on top of me, and I peppered her with kisses, inspired, remembering the Litany of the Blessed Virgin as we rolled over the floor, kissing now her neck, now her knee, her leg, her elbow, anything within range of my lips as I cried, 'Mystical Rose! Seat of Wisdom! Cause of Joy! Vessel of Honor! Tower of David! Tower of Ivory! Refuge

of Sinners! Ark of the Covenant! Gate of Heaven! Morning
Star! Comforter of the afflicted! Help of Christians! Lamb
of God!'

Squirming and pulling, she dragged me this way and that
across the glossy floor, her shoes off, belting me wildly with
both hands, then getting to her feet, tearing out strands
of my hair, finally breaking free. For some moments we
panted in silence, getting our breaths, she leaning agaisnt
the refrigerator, I on my stomach.

Finally she spoke. 'Will you kindly go home now?'

She tucked in her blouse, smoothed her skirt, and stepped
into her shoes. I stood up and began shoving my shirt tail
and it fell there at my feet — her golden panties with the
black sequins. I picked them up. I was beyond shame. I just
held them, wearily, gasping for breath.

'My new pants!' she said.

'Can I have them?'

'No!'

'Please.'

'Of course not!' She snatched them from my grasp. 'What
a terrible boy you are!'

'I love you,' I said, my arms out.

'Don't you dare!'

I stared at her long neck, her yellow hair, the miracle
of how she stood in her shoes, and I started to cry, for
Dorothy Parrish would never be mine, nobody who came
from Torricella Peligna ever possessed a girl like Dorothy
Parrish, not in a thousand years, not as long as there was
another man on earth.

'I mean it,' I sobbed. 'I can't help it. I love you.'

'Please,' she said quietly.

She crossed to the back door and opened it, and I picked up my mackinaw and walked past her and out on the service porch.

'Good night,' she said.

'You'll be sorry,' I told her as I put on the mackinaw. 'You'll hear about me some day, and you'll be sorry.'

She closed the door and the lock clicked. I went down the driveway to the street.

Chapter Four

Two blocks down College Avenue I ran into Kenny on his way home from the show. He said, 'Hi, lover.'

'Aren't you cute.'

'You missed a great show. Both pictures. Ginger Rogers – what a body.'

'I have to tell you something about me and your sister.'

'Don't tell me you scored.' He was mocking me.

'I kissed her, that's all.'

'Was it that bad? You look like a fugitive from justice.'

'I liked it. She didn't.'

'She's too old for you. Not your type.'

'What's my type, Mr Anthony?'

'She'll emerge out of your fame, some girl along the way. Maybe a movie star like Ginger Rogers. It's not important now. You have to think of the arm, Dom. Nothing matters but the arm.'

'The Arm's not worried.' I held it out. 'The Arm knows what's important.'

'Does it know that women and pitching don't mix?'

'It's not so sure.'

'Does it pine for a certain tropical setting off the coast of California, owned by a chewing gum tycoon?'

'The Arm is aware of such a place.'

'Ask it, when do we leave?'

'Pretty soon.'

'Time's running out. Let's move.'

He stood pink-cheeked under the lamp post, warm as a beaver inside his new coat, his feet in heavy galoshes, confident, free to go anywhere.

'You talk pretty big,' I said. 'Are you by any chance the son of Joe Parrish, one of the richest men in this town?'

'Oh, balls! There you go again.' He kicked at the snow. 'A lousy fifty bucks. You can raise it, if you try.'

'How?'

'Your old man.'

'He hasn't got it.'

'Can't he borrow it?'

'He wouldn't ask.'

'How do you know?'

'I just know.'

He smiled faintly. 'You know what I think, Guinea? I think you're chicken.'

I thought of hitting him, but suddenly his smile was his sister's, and so were his placid eyes. I spat right in his face. He did not move, the spittle trickling down his nose as he calmly flicked it away with the back of his glove.

'Feel better now?' he said.

Shoving my fists into the mackinaw, I walked away, but after twenty steps I slowed down. I liked him. He was the only friend I had. He respected The Arm. Sometimes he needled me, but I did the same to him, and we had a common dream. I couldn't throw it all away. He was trudging up the hill, bending forward against the incline.

'Ken!'

He turned around.

'Sorry.'

'It's okay, pal.'

'You sore?'

'Nope.'

'See you at the Elks tomorrow.'

'Talk to your old man, Dom. It won't hurt to try.'

'Okay.'

It was payday at the pottery works, so the Onyx Bar was swirling with customers two deep along the bar and four or five in every booth. The floor was slick and wet from tramped-in snow and spilled beer, and the juke box played deafening country music, everybody shouting to be heard over it. Riley the bartender saw me enter and yelled, 'He's not here, Don,' which wasn't my name.

I squirmed my way between the bar and the booths to the poolroom in back. Everything was quiet back there, no players at the pool tables, but a crowd of men at the two poker games to the rear. My father wasn't there. I crossed to the cue rack. Sometimes the old man went out of town to shoot pool, taking his own cue along. But his stick was there, locked in the rack, his name burned into the handle.

I left the big room and started back through the crowd at the bar when a woman's hand darted from one of the booths and plucked my sleeve. It was a plump, cigarette browned hand with two gold rings on the fingers. It was Rita Calabrese. She was alone in the booth, sipping sweet wine. You could smell the sweetness when she spoke.

'You're Mary Molise's boy.'

She had known my mother when they were girls together in Denver. Her husband Ralph owned Studebaker Rockne

Motors, and she had a son Robert who once wrestled Strangler Lewis in Greeley. My mother said she was a bad woman.

I asked her if she had seen my father.

'Sit down,' she said. 'I adore your mother. She's an angel.'

The moment I sat down Riley shouted, 'On your way, Don,' and jerked his thumb toward the door. I started to leave and Rita took my sleeve again.

'You know Edna Pruitt?' she asked.

'Sure. What of it?'

'What do *you* think?'

'My father's with her?'

'I didn't say that,' she smirked. 'All I said was, I think your mother's an angel.'

You had to be from out of town not to know Edna Pruitt. Years before she had been charged with performing abortions and there had been a famous trial in which she was acquitted. But her sinister reputation lingered on, and every new generation of Roper kids claimed to have found stillborn embryos in the garbage can behind Edna Pruitt's house. Many a time I too had paused, furtive and fearful, to lift the lid of her garbage can and peer inside, repulsed and expecting something awful. I was always disappointed.

Her white frame bungalow was on Pine Street, across from the new post office. On the door of the glassed in front porch was the sign:

> Edna Mae Pruitt, DSC, PHM
> Chiropractic Masseuse
> Personalized Manipulation
> Spiritual Healing
> Day or Night. Phone 37 W

The front of the house was in darkness, but a light shone behind the green shade at one of the side windows. I stood in the street and wondered: what the hell am I doing here? If I wanted my father's help, and he was in there, the last place I should be was near this house. In the bitter cold the sky heaved a quiet sigh and it began to snow.

I looked at the lighted window again. Was he in there? What was he doing? It was none of my business, but I had to know. Maybe they were having an orgy, committing adultery. What would I do — stop them? And be carried off mangled and broken to the morgue? Roper boy murder victim. Father knifes son ... Police find murder weapon in snow ... Distraught father held ... Blames uncontrollable temper ... Was good boy, parent states ... Prominent athlete ... Heartbroken father tries to hang self in cell ... Priest eulogizes murdered youth ... Destined for major leagues, says Father Murray ... Team mates act as pallbearers ... Jury finds Molise guilty ... Execution date set ... Governor denies last minute plea ... Bricklayer executed.

I crossed the small lawn to the window and peered through an inch of light under the green shade. It wasn't any orgy, and it wasn't a party. It didn't even look like a love tryst. It was just two people, Papa and Edna Pruitt, sitting quietly in the parlor, under a big picture of President Hoover. Edna was in a rocking chair, knitting a sock, and my father sat at a bridge table playing solitaire. He hadn't even taken off his coat, but there was something peaceful about him, a strange serenity I had never seen before.

Edna was ten years older, a heavy woman in the white uniform of a nurse, down to white stockings and white shoes. They did not speak or look at one another, and they were motionless except for their hands, my father slowly turning cards, Edna's fingers working the knitting needles. If he had not been my father, I would have sworn they had been married for twenty years, two people sharing silence and companionship on a Winter night.

Then my father yawned and stretched his arms. Edna yawned too, smiled, and crossed to the closet, the weight of her thick body making the floor creak. She brought out my father's overcoat and held it open as he put his arms into it. Then the most dramatic incident of the night took place: Edna kissed him. She kissed him on the jawbone, casually, and he started for the door.

As he stepped out on the porch, I dashed up the alley, staying a little ahead of him, and we met on Twelfth Street. Out of breath, I got in stride with him.

'Where you been, at this hour?'

'With Kenny. I want to talk to you, Papa. It's very important.'

'I thought it was settled. You're going to finish school, then come to work for me.'

'It won't work.'

'Shut up about it.'

We went along stride for stride, the snow piling up on our coats. I decided on a different approach.

'You know who Joe DiMaggio is, Papa? And Tony Lazzeri, and Frank Crosetti?'

'Ball players,' he groused.

'You ever heard of Babe Pinelli, or Lou Fonseca, or Ron Pelligrini?'

'More ball players.'

'Or Vic Monte, or Sam La Torra, or Boots Zarlingo?'

'Ball players.'

'People, Papa! Human beings like you and me. Sons of tailors and butchers and fishermen. Of barbers and coal miners. Italian-Americans from homes like ours, from all over the country in this land of opportunity. You know what they say about opportunity, Papa?'

'You know everything. Tell me.'

'It knocks but once.'

He stopped and so did I. He looked at me in exasperation, his hand sliding from the pocket of his coat. He doubled it into a fist and brought it close to my nose.

'See this? It knocks too. Just once.'

But I had to make my stand.

'I'm leaving town, Papa.'

He turned and walked on, faster. We went a block before he spoke.

'Where you going?'

'California.'

He stopped once more, his hat and shoulders coated with snow. 'And you're gonna get rich, playing ball.'

'I'm going to try out with the Chicago Cubs.'

'Do the Chicago Cubs know this?'

'They'll know, when they see me.'

Pain and sadness softened his face. He put his hand on my shoulder, hesitant to speak what was on his mind. But I knew.

'Say it. You don't think I'm good enough.'

'You're good enough, Kid,' he said gently. 'But you're not *tough* enough. You know what I'm talking about? Those men are like iron. They're hard, tough. They'll grind you in the dirt. They'll kill you. They'll break your heart.'

We were on this dead street in the middle of the night in snow so thick we could hardly see one another, and he was telling me I was weak, my own father, and it depressed me to realize he was judging me on the basis of himself. He was a great bricklayer and a failure; I was a great ball player and I would fail too. Like father, like son. With this difference: he was from Torricella Peligna, a foreigner, and I wasn't.

'You don't understand me at all,' I said, and that closed the subject, and I was relieved. How was I to get fifty dollars from this poor, rumpled stranger from so far away, floundering around in a big, complicated, new country? Stone, goats, bread, wine: he understood those things. Not baseball.

We slogged on, crossing the bridge that spanned Roper Creek, where he paused, pleased to find a cigar butt that had fallen through a hole in the lining of his overcoat pocket. I waited for him to light up and smelled the fragrance of the cigar in the heavy air.

'Look,' he said, pointing with the match.

Through the high snow along the creek bank, a beaver dragged an aspen branch. We watched the little creature splash into the water and swim to the beginnings of a new dam.

'That's what I mean,' he said. 'Weather like this, everybody works but the bricklayer. Even chipmunks.'

'Beaver. Not chipmunk.'

'Chipmunks, too.'

He shouted to the beaver: 'Try using mortar sometime! You'll see!'

We stood on the bridge whose piers my father had erected brick on brick. I remembered the summer three years ago when the job was in progress, and the place where his little concrete mixer had stood on the creek bank, the engine putt-putting through the long, warm day.

We plodded on. The first building beyond the bridge was Hale's Candy Store. Every brick in its walls had passed through my father's hands. Beneath our feet under the snow was the concrete sidewalk my father had poured and smoothed with his trowels.

How many things he had built when the sun gave him a chance! All over town you could see his handiwork — schools, churches, homes, garages, chimneys, driveways, terraces, fireplaces, sidewalks of stone, of concrete, of brick, steps going up and steps going down.

Work, sweat, paycheck. How he loved his task, like that tireless mixer of his, the Jaeger, his partner, wheezing and snorting through all those good days. Then the rains came, or the snow fell, and the machine was trundled away to the shed and covered with a canvas, out of work like his partner. No wonder he went to see Edna Pruitt. He was not a machine made of iron, hibernating under a canvas, sitting out the winter. He was flesh and blood.

Poor old Papa. What a life! But not Dom Molise. I had a way out, a gift of God, The Arm. As we stood on the front porch knocking the snow from our shoes, my mind reached out suddenly to trap the solution to my problem. I had found a way. I knew what had to be done.

Chapter Five

Next morning I ditched school and hurried over to Roper High to tell Kenny my plan. I had to catch him before his first class, so I stationed myself at the top of the school steps, watching the flow of students coming off the street.

Last night's storm was over, and a sweet day it was, the sun nice and warm, storm clouds on the run. The snow melted fast, brewing torrents of brown water roaring down the curbs. Beyond the Rockies to the West the sky sparkled a Virgin Mary blue, reminding me that somewhere out there the Chicago Cubs were probably having breakfast at that very moment.

The Cubs! My future team mates: Manager Joe McCarthy, Charley Grimm, Hack Wilson, Bill Nicholson, Gabby Hartnett, Stan Hack.

'Gabby, how's that Molise kid doing?'

'Jesus, he's fantastic.'

'Cocky kid.'

'You'd be too, if you was him.'

'He finally signed his contract.'

'Thank God. What'd he get?'

'Twenty thousand, with a five thousand bonus.'

'Lotta moola for a seventeen year old.'

'For a twenty-five game winner? Hell, we stole him.'

The nine o'clock bell clanged as a bus pulled up and Kenny got out with a gang of kids. They raced up the stairs. Seeing me there startled Kenny.

'What's up?'

'You ready to go?' I said.

'Catalina?'

'We can leave today.'

'You raise the dough?'

'I'll have it in three hours.' I took his arm. 'Let's get some coffee and talk.'

He hung back. 'I got an English class.'

'That's for kids. Today we become men.'

He followed me across the street to the corner drugstore and we mounted a couple of stools. As we smoked and drank coffee I told him about my father's concrete mixer and how I planned to borrow it. There was a builder's supply store in Longmont, ten miles away, where I could get fifty, maybe sixty dollars for the mixer.

'Once it's sold, we grab the five o'clock bus and it's California all the way.'

He was not enthusiastic, drumming the marbletop counter, swirling coffee around in his mouth, swallowing thoughtfully.

'Where's the mixer now?'

'In the shed behind our house. We'll need a truck to haul it away. That's where you come in.'

'Isn't that known as stealing?'

'How can a man steal from his own father? It's like community property. What's his is mine, and vice versa.'

'That might be true if you owned anything, which you don't.'

'Not now,' I agreed, having rehearsed all the answers. 'But in a couple of months I'll be able to buy him a brand new mixer, one of those super jobs.'

'What makes you so sure?'

'I'll be playing ball for money.'

He squeezed shut his eyes and shook his head.

'Madness,' he said. 'Madness.'

His pessimism was getting me down.

'What's the matter with you?' I said. 'Who's chicken now?'

'I'm not chicken. I'm not a thief either.'

'Thief? What thief? All you do is borrow your old man's truck so we haul the mixer to Longmont.'

'That makes me an accessory to the crime.'

'Crime, thief, stealing! Stop talking like that! You think my father's going to let the loan of a broken-down concrete-mixer stand in the way of my whole future?'

'Knowing your father, yes.'

He was so calm, so grave, so stubborn I wanted to strangle him, but I tried reasoning with him instead.

'Look, stupid. Don't you see how foolish it would be to *ask* for my father's permission to sell the mixer? You *know* he'd refuse.'

'That's what I mean.'

'Okay, stupid. But if I *don't* ask him, and sell the mixer anyway, what can he do? He'll *have* to say yes, since the deed was done. And a yes is a yes, before or after. Don't you understand what I'm saying? In other words, I'm not *stealing* the mixer, I'm merely taking it out of the shed and putting it to use for a while, borrowing it for a few weeks while it just sits there rusting up, doing nothing. After I sign with the Cubs, I send the old boy a few hundred bucks and he goes out and buys himself a brand new mixer, and he still has some extra cash in his pocket. In other words, for the use of the mixer which is just laying there in the shed, he makes five or six hundred percent profit. And while this is going on, I'm playing regular ball and mailing my mother a check each week. She pays off our debts, it's summertime and my father's pulling down big jobs on account of his new mixer, which can do the work of five men, which is how it is when you have the proper equipment. So everybody's happy. What's wrong with that? Are you against happiness, Ken? Are you against my family getting ahead in the world? Why should my old man stay poor, while yours gets rich? Do you have something against us because we're Italians? Have I ever stooped to borrowing anything from you? Am I asking *you* to loan me the money? No. All I'm asking from you is the loan of the truck, so that I can borrow my father's mixer for a few weeks. If that's asking too much, forget it, forget our friendship, let's shake hands and go our separate ways.'

He sat there silently, frowning and full of doubts, rubbing the back of his neck.

'For the sake of argument, suppose, just suppose you don't make it with the Cubs? It's possible. Anything's possible.'

It shocked me. 'Some friend!' I said. 'One day I'm God's gift to baseball, and now I'm a Cub reject! All these months, building me up, and now it comes out in the open: the betrayal, the knife in the back!' I looked at him in disgust. 'That's all, buster. That finishes us!'

I slammed a nickel on the counter and walked out. He ran up the street after me.

'Okay,' he said. 'I'll get the truck, on one condition.'

'What condition?'

'That you'll pay your father back, either with the money you earn from baseball, or any other job.'

'What "other" job?'

'Laying brick, maybe.'

'I'm a ball player, Parrish. A pro. People pay me to pitch. That's the way I earn my money.'

'Not yet, you don't,' he said stubbornly.

I took him by the arm to the bus bench on the corner and told him to sit down. Once more I called upon the reserves of my patience to explain certain elemental facts. It was possible, of course, that I wouldn't make the Cubs. Many things could divert me – a broken leg, a fatal disease, an automobile accident. But even these were only temporary setbacks beyond my control. The possibility also existed that the Cub management had no need for another left hander, which would necessitate sending me down to one of their minor league clubs, perhaps L.A. in the Pacific Coast League, or Atlanta in the Southern Association. But that was as low as I could sink. I knew that, The Arm knew it, Kenny knew it.

'Right?'

He shrugged vaguely. 'I guess so.'

'Don't guess, Ken. You're fooling with a human life.'

'Okay,' he sighed. 'You're right.'

So it was stealing, so it was wrong. Was it as wrong as my father two-timing my mother? Did he imagine I was some punk kid who didn't know or care that he was dishonoring his marriage? Did he believe he could go unpunished? I resolved the first dollar I earned would go to my mother. I'd get her a lawyer. I'd get her out of Roper, in a little house of her own. I'd even support my father, send him a few bucks a week so he wouldn't have to work, but he'd have to live alone, in a hotel.

At the hardware store Ken told his father that he needed the truck to move some gym equipment for coach, and Mr Parrish gave him the keys to the pick-up. We drove up Arapahoe and turned into our alley, making fresh tire furrows in the flawless snow. We reached the shed behind our house, and I jumped out and opened the tin doors. The square, corrugated iron building was piled with planks, mortar boards, sacks of cement and stacks of brick. It was fifty feet from the house, the path to the back porch buried under two feet of snow, a solitary place in winter, scarcely noticed, never visited.

I signalled directions to Kenny as he backed the truck into the shed, a few inches from the concrete mixer. He cut the engine and looked around nervously.

'What if your old man shows up?' he whispered.

'He never comes back here. Nobody does.'

To prove it, I picked up a piece of pipe and banged it against the mixer, a thundering clatter that shook the building.

Frantic, he gasped, 'Good God, don't!'

He rushed to the only window in the building, curtained with cobwebs, giving a murky view of the back yard. 'Let's get this evil thing over with,' he said.

We examined the mixer. It was a real antique, maybe fifteen years old, on two large iron wheels, with a tongue and hitch. We secured the tongue to a hitch on the rear bumper of the truck, chaining it firmly. Then I opened the engine housing and peeled off the certificate of ownership pasted inside the door. Lifting the Parker pen from Ken's sweater, I signed my father's name on the transfer-of-ownership line.

Ken caught his breath.

'God, that's a cold-blooded forgery!'

'Forgery, hell. Isn't my name Molise? I'm just changing my first name.'

Sweat glistened on his forehead and he was breathing hard, his eyes flashing toward the small window.

'You're not even human,' he said. 'You're an animal. I ought to call the cops.'

'The end justifies the means.'

'Bullshit, you thief.'

'Let's go,' I said. 'Quick.'

He was reluctant, wanting to quit right there, but I slapped my hands energetically. 'All set!' I said.

He climbed into the truck and started the engine. I stood aside, watching the hitch as the wheels turned and the truck moved out into the alley, the mixer clattering after it. Closing the shed doors, I got in beside him. Jaws clamped, he stared straight ahead.

He was about to shift gears when a small, dark, wrinkled face shrouded in a black shawl peered above our back gate. It was Grandma Bettina. For a quick moment I thought I was in Torricella Peligna. I could see the town behind her, the cobbled streets, the crumbling stone houses, the church, with old black crones making their way up the stairs.

'Oh, my God!' Kenny said.

'Move!'

He couldn't. He was frozen with shame, his breathing stopped, his eyes bulging, his knuckles iced up on the steering wheel. The gate creaked as Grandma pushed it open and stepped into the alley. In dreadful fascination Kenny watched her through the side mirror as she circled the mixer, examining the way it was secured to the truck.

'How awful,' he moaned. 'How fucking awful!' He closed his eyes and methodically banged his forehead against the steering wheel. But it wasn't awful. It was preposterous. It was farcical, insane. I started to laugh. The last, the remotest eventuality, and there she was, my old Grandma, nodding her head in full awareness of what was going on.

Through snow above her knees, she waded to the front of the truck and looked up at Kenny. There was no surprise in her manner. She seemed to accept what she saw, resigned to it as she spoke in Italian.

'So this is the American way,' she said. 'To kill the soul of a man, and then chop off his hands. What will my son do without this machine? Do you expect him to mix mortar with a hoe?'

Ken couldn't look at her. 'What's that?' he asked. 'Tell me what she said.'

'She says it's a pile of junk, and she's glad we're hauling it away.'

'You're a liar.'

There was no hiding it. The evil of the deed was pinned to that moment of the day, to the angle of the sun in the sky, to the crystal brilliance of the melting snow, the drift of clouds beyond the mountains, the shadow cast by the shed, the bleak resignation in Grandma's eyes.

'Steal if you must,' a sob in her voice. 'From banker, from the light company, from the tax collector, but spare the unhappy fruit of my womb.'

'What's that?' Ken asked. 'What'd she say?'

I told him it was hard to translate. 'A kind of Italian saying.'

He leaped to the ground.

'I'm through! I've had it! When you're finished, bring the truck back to the store.' He crossed to Grandma, his hands imploring her. 'Look, Grandma. I'm clean. I've got nothing to do with this, capeach? You savvy?' He touched his chest. 'Me no guilty. Me good man.' Pointing at me, 'Him bad man. Me no steal. Me, friend. Him, crook.'

He hurried away down the alley, his feet retracing the grooves of the truck tires in the snow. I climbed into the truck. I could feel my skull cracking as the old eyes drilled it. Looking straight ahead, I heard her speak of first and last things, of birth and death, of crime and damnation, of Judas and the fall of honor among sons. The roar of the engine drowned out her words as I shifted gears and drove away. Through the rearview mirror I saw her black, lonely figure in the alley, her hands fluttering to the sky.

The quickest route to Longmont was past the fair grounds and through the cemetery to the main highway, which avoided traffic through town. Everybody knew my father's mixer, so I kept off the main traveled streets and stayed in alleys until I reached the fair grounds, the mixer clattering along like a load of tin cans.

Entering the cemetery, my troubles began, for the only road wound past the grave of my grandfather, Giovanni Molise. It troubled me even before I drove into the graveyard, thinking of it and boiling up courage to confront it.

Then I saw the granite cross on the stone pedestal marking the grave. It was tall as a man and very slender, cloaked with snow, as if it wore a white shawl. The monument was my father's pride and joy. Off and on for two years he had worked on it in our shed, reducing a huge chunk of marble into the graceful cross, chipping and polishing the stone until it was as smooth as human skin.

The noise was responsible, the clatter and banging of the mixer shattering the graveyard quiet. The thought of driving past the cross filled me with dread. Fifty feet away, I stopped the truck and considered other ways to avoid the passage. But I was in a forest of monuments, and the only way around was by driving over the graves of a hundred other poor souls at peace there.

Not that I expected any trouble from my grandfather, for he was dead seven years, but the memory of him was still above the ground. Had he stood there alive, I could have defied him as easily as I had his wife in our alley. But he was dead, terribly dead, and I was afraid of his helplessness. I remembered how he used to be when he was on the earth, with fish lures in his crumpled canvas hat, a lover of walnuts and sunflower seeds, how beautifully he sharpened knives, the way he walked railroad tracks from town to town with the heavy whetstone wheel strapped to his back. I remembered how he always sat on his haunches and poked the ground with a stick, not a learned man but a scholar who smiled all the time, pleased to be just a human being in the world.

How could I pass? How low had I sunk? The lure of fame and fortune had turned me into a madman. Was this to be Grandpa's reward for coming all the way from Abruzzi, so that his grandson should blight his grave with stolen goods?

I eased the truck forward a few feet so that I could look at the inscription chiseled on the pedestal.

GIOVANNI MOLISE
1853–1926
REQUIESCAT IN PACE

Go back, The Arm said, turn this thing around, you fool, before I drop off; turn around and go back and forget Catalina, lay brick with your father, dig ditches, be a bum if you must, but turn away from this wickedness.

I swung the truck around and started for home.

Driving into our alley, I saw my father standing beside the shed. He did not seem angry, simply staring as I pulled up.

'Hi,' I said.

He stared a moment longer, then opened the shed doors. I backed the mixer into the shed and he stared some more. He stared as I turned off the engine and jumped to the ground.

'I'll explain everything,' I said.

He stared as I went back to the hitch and removed the chain. 'I was thinking about buying you a new mixer,' I told him. 'I wanted to find out what kind of a trade-in they'd make on this pile of junk.'

As he removed his overcoat and hung it on a nail, I went on: 'Since we're going to be partners this summer, I thought now was a good time to get us some new equipment. No sense in bucking competition with obsolete machinery.'

Beneath his overcoat was an unmatched suit coat which he also peeled off. 'Then I thought maybe I should consult you first. After all, you're the head man in this operation.'

He stepped over to the truck and rapped the fender lightly with his knuckle. 'You steal this too?' he asked.

I explained that Kenny had borrowed the truck from his father.

'What's this?' he said, reaching out and snatching the pink owner's certificate protruding from my sweater pocket. He unfolded the document and studied it, more white showing in his eyes.

'You don't even know how to steal good,' he said with a shake of his head. 'You forged my name on the wrong line.'

I smiled. 'You're all wrong. Would I be here, if I tried to forge your name? Did I steal anything? What did I steal? The mixer? It's right here, where it always is. I resent these wild charges.'

He was staring again. With the shed doors open I thought of making a run for the alley. He would chase me a block or two, but he would never catch me. Suddenly his right hand shot out and slapped me across the face, and he was dancing like a fighter, his fists poised, a cloud of coal dust boiling up around his churning feet.

'Defend yourself!' he ordered, bobbing about on his toes, feinting and jabbing and circling. I just stood there, surprised, not fighting back. I could never fight him, never. I backed away, avoiding the jabs.

'God damn it, fight!' he snarled.

'What for?'

'If you can steal from me, you can fight me. Come on, hit me!'

A sudden jab caught me at the side of the nose. Pain, like glass shattering, quick and blinding. The taste of blood. I covered my nose and felt the warm ooze of blood through my fingers. He gasped in dismay, struck himself on the cheek.

'Mama mia!'

He rushed into the alley and plunged his hands into the snow and hurried back with two dripping handsful, holding them toward my face. I pressed my nose into the mound of snow and in moments the bleeding was over, my face wet and cold. He pulled out a blue handkerchief with white dots and I used it to wipe my face. He was pale, his hand trembling as he carefully traced a finger along the bridge of my nose.

'I'm okay,' I told him.

'Why?' he implored. 'You're no thief – why?'

Maybe the bloody nose was responsible, but for once we stopped being father and son and became friends, and I was able to tell him of my hopes and despairs, the boredom of poverty, the chance to leave home and try my hand at pro ball. He lit a cigar and walked to the door, his back to me, and I spilled out my dream as clouds of smoke filled the shed.

When he turned to face me there was no anger or disappointment in his face, but a softness, a desire to understand and sympathize.

'Wait a year,' he said quietly. 'Finish high school, then go.'

'I want to go now!'

'You won't listen. You want it your way and nothing else. It shows how young you are.'

'I want to help you, Papa. Send money home. You can throw away that overcoat, buy some new clothes.'

He studied me, frowning, wheels turning in his head. 'How do you know you're good enough?'

'Because I'm a natural born pitcher.'

He pulled and squeezed his face, trying to extract a decision. 'I don't know. I want to do the right thing. I'll talk to somebody.'

'Who?'

'I don't know. How much do you need?'

'Fifty.'

He whistled, shook his head bleakly. 'It's no good. It's a trap I'm in. I'm wrong if I do, I'm wrong if I don't.'

I didn't care where he got the money. Let it come from Edna Pruitt, for all I cared. He'd get it back, I'd see to that. When the Cubs offered me a contract, I'd insist on a bonus to cover such details. Maybe an extra thousand.

We drove uptown in the pickup. He liked the truck. For years he had wanted one of his own. Whenever there was a new job he had to hire Chet's Hauling to move his materials.

'Nice car,' he said, studying the cab.

'In a couple of months you'll have one just like it,' I told him. 'Only it'll be brand new, with your name on the side: Molise Construction Company.'

'Cut it out, kid. What do you know about the world?'

'Who needs the world? Just give me baseball.'

He sighed, depressed, his face full of pain. I pulled up in front of the Onyx and he got out.

'You won't fail me, Papa. Of all the people in the world, you're the one I depend on.'

'We'll see. I'll talk to somebody.'

'Thanks for giving me this chance.'

He screamed at me: 'Cut it out, you hear? Cut it out.'

He slammed the car door and hurried inside the Onyx. I drove the truck back to the hardware store and parked it in back. Mr Parrish opened the back door as I stepped down. He walked around the truck, inspecting it carefully. His cold eyes settled on me.

'Don't ever let me catch you driving this truck again savvy?'

'I had Ken's permission.'

'Drop dead,' he said.

I wasn't worried about the money anymore. One way or another, my father would put his hands on it and in a matter of hours Ken and I would be on our way. Walking across town to Roper High, I had the clean, sweet feeling I would never walk those streets again. No more bitterness, no painful memories. It had been a good town, a fine place to launch a career. Nothing spectacular like New York or Chicago, just a nice solid little town that produced a great ballplayer.

I found Kenny in the drug store across the street from school. It was noon and the place swarmed with kids having lunch. We went outside in the sun. He was grim and not friendly until I told him what happened to the mixer.

'I didn't sell it. I took it back.'

'It's there now?' he asked, his face brightening. 'Does Grandma know?'

'Sure, she does.'

'Thank God!' He almost went into a dance as he threw his arms around me. Then I told him the big news: that my father had okayed the trip to California and was now raising the money. With a grin he put both hands on my shoulders.

'Dom, you did a great thing, taking that mixer back. You've got real integrity.'

'It was quite a struggle,' I admitted. 'A weaker man would have gone through with it.'

'It took a lot of guts.'

'Well . . .'

'I'm proud of you for saving our friendship. I was ready to brush you off.'

'Dorothy, too, I'll bet.'

'No question about it. She hates weakness.'

The old flame rekindled, sparked up, and I said, 'Ken, do me a favor.'

'Name it, Iron Man.'

'Tell her what I did. I think she'd like to hear it.'

'That's a promise.'

To everybody's surprise, Papa showed up for supper. Mama had fixed a casserole of lamb kidneys cooked in parsley and wine, and after my father's third helping she was ecstatic and dashed into the bedroom to put on a fresh apron and a piece of ribbon in her hair. She nervously began to gather the dishes, even though we hadn't finished eating. Augie hung on to his plate.

'Oh, you've had enough,' she laughed, and took the plate away.

My father refused to look at me. After the table was cleared and the others had left, I sat across from him as he finished his wine. Still avoiding my eyes, he groped for something inside his shirt pocket and thrust his fist toward me.

'Here.'

I felt a roll of greenbacks in my palm and caught my breath. It seemed a fortune. I left the table and went out on the front porch to count the money.

They were greasy dollar bills, as if gathered a dollar here and a dollar there. I counted them with a sense of rising calamity, then counted them again. There were twenty-five. It had to be a mistake. They felt simply colossal. I was counting them a third time when my father stepped out on the porch.

'It's the best I could do,' he said.

It wasn't enough. The bus fare alone was twenty-four dollars to Los Angeles, but I couldn't bring myself to say anything. He had tried, had done his best. Looking at him, his tired face, his wet eyes, I knew he had been through a terrible ordeal.

I thanked him, but he guessed my thoughts.

'What about the Parrish boy?' he suggested. 'He's got the money. Maybe he'll loan you, till you get started.'

'Maybe.'

He gazed at the silent street, the naked trees dripping in the warm night. 'I went through hell for that money. Now use it. Go play ball. And send money home.'

I pushed the bills into my pocket.

'Don't worry, Papa. You'll never regret it.'

He turned and smiled, his horny paw circling my arm. 'Make a muscle.'

'Wrong arm,' I said. 'Try this one.' I turned the left arm toward him. 'Get a good grip.'

His fingers took hold.

'Harder.'

His fingers dug deeply like bands of steel. Slowly I bent The Arm until a mighty bulge tore his grip asunder. He almost laughed.

'Pretty good.'

'That's just raw power. You should see what happens to a baseball.'

'Remember. Send money home.'

*   *   *

I knew I could count on Kenny. He had a regular weekly allowance and a bank account, and besides, it wasn't quite like being flat broke and asking him to finance the whole trip.

From the street I saw the light in his window, so I knew he was home. Light bloomed in Dorothy's window too, and I hoped it would be she who opened the door when I rang the bell, and not Kenny.

It wasn't Kenny either. It was Mr Parrish.

'I want to talk to you,' he said, quickly stepping out on the porch and closing the door. He was like a piece of ice. He tried to keep his voice frozen too, but it trembled with emotion.

'I want you to stay away from my son,' he said. 'And stay away from this house.' His finger jabbed my chest. 'Is that clear? You're not welcome here.' He was shaking.

'What's wrong with you?' I said.

'Now, listen. Kenny's not going on this stupid junket. Those are my orders. And he's not to associate with you anymore. You're a bad influence on the boy, understand? So leave him alone. Stay away from here, clear away on your side of town, or I'll call the police.'

Before I could speak, and I had nothing to say, he rushed inside, bolted the door loudly, and turned off the porch light. I walked away in a daze. I knew Mr Parrish didn't like me very well, but not that he hated me. Was it because I had driven his truck? Had Ken told him about the mixer? Did he know what happened between Dorothy and me? I didn't know.

I didn't know anything, the time of day, my ass from a hot rock, who I was, or why, and all at once, trudging down the hill toward home, I didn't care, I was tired of caring, and in his way Mr Parrish had made the decision for me. The trip was off. No Kenny, no trip. I was too stupid to make it alone, I might go the wrong way, end up in Torricella Peligna, where I belonged. My father was right. I should wait a year. Hell, Roper wasn't such a bad town. At least I could walk around in it without getting lost. I would return the money to my father and wait another year.

The Arm began to protest, twitching, crying like a spoiled child, calling me chicken, a welcher. You crumb, you creep, all you think about is yourself. I gave it a consoling pat. Look, I said, there's plenty of time, let's finish our education and have a nice summer right here in Roper. We'll work for the old man, pitch on Sundays, and save our money. But The Arm didn't care for that kind of talk. It got flabby and listless and pretended it was dead. I had to smile. What a sly one!

Turning up our street past Art's Service Station, I saw something familiar in the open garage that served as a grease rack. I crossed the asphalt for a closer look. And there it was, my father's concrete mixer, the engine dismantled, the parts spread on the floor, the carburetor soaking in a bucket of gasoline.

I had a sudden pain in my chest, a feeling that I was going to cry. Over my shoulder I saw Art Belden, the station owner, leaning back in a chair, listening to Bing Crosby singing, 'Where the Blue of the Night' over the radio. I walked over and opened the door, and Art said, 'Hi, Dom.'

His open lunch pail was on the desk in front of him. He was dressed in white coveralls with four pencils in the chest pocket, and I hated him. I hated the precision neatness of the peanut butter sandwiches he was eating, the crusts daintily cut away by his wife. I hated her too. I hated the snug grey bungalow they lived in on Spruce Street. I hated his Collie dog. I hated his amiable smile, and I hated his answer before I even asked what my father's mixer was doing in his garage.

'It *used* to be your father's,' he said. 'I bought it this afternoon.'

I believed him, and I said, 'I don't believe you.'

He bit into his sandwich, turned off Bing Crosby, and handed me the bill of sale, signed by my father. For the twenty-five greasy dollars in my pocket.

'I'll buy it back.'

'It's not for sale.'

'I'll give you thirty.'

He shook his head and poured milk into a cup from his thermos.

'Make it forty.'

'Look. I don't want to sell it.'

I pulled out the wad of bills and tossed it on the desk. 'Fifty bucks. Twenty-five now, and twenty-five this summer.'

A car drove up and he went out to service it. I picked up the roll of money and walked back to the mixer. It was beat up and banged like my father's hands, a part of his life, so strangely ancient, as if from a far country, from Torricella Peligna. I put my arms around it and kissed it with my mouth and cried for my father and all fathers, and sons too, for being alive in that time, for myself, because I had to go to California now, I had no choice, I had to make good.